Things don't feel right here.

I want to open my eyes in the morn[...] wallpaper with the tiny blue flowe[...] Aunt Patty does not believe in putting up wallpaper, not even in the bathroom. She says mold grows behind it.

I want Mom to read to us for an hour before bedtime, all of us in a clump like alligators in the sun so we can all look at the pictures together. Aunt Patty tucks us into bed before it is even full dark. We want our mom. We're worried about her having to sleep all alone. We worry that she doesn't eat right, now that she doesn't have us to feed. We miss her.

I hear Aunt Patty's bossy voice, rousing Uncle Hob out of his bed. She's telling him he has to come outside to order us down. Or to plead with us, whichever he thinks will work. That sad feeling I have hardens into a mad feeling and I don't think I'll ever get down off this roof. I'll stay here till kingdom comes.

———◆———

getting

near

to

baby

AUDREY COULOUMBIS

SCHOLASTIC INC.
New York Toronto London Auckland Sydney
Mexico City New Delhi Hong Kong Buenos Aires

ISBN 0-439-37651-3

Copyright © 1999 by Audrey Couloumbis.
All rights reserved.
Published by Scholastic Inc., 555 Broadway, New York, NY 10012,
by arrangement with Puffin Books, a division of Penguin Putnam Inc.
SCHOLASTIC and associated logos are trademarks and/or
registered trademarks of Scholastic Inc.

12 11 10 9 8 7 6 5   4 5 6/0

Printed in the U.S.A.   40

First Scholastic paperback printing, December 2001

ACKNOWLEDGMENTS

There are some things a writer can be lucky enough to have, like friends who really want it to happen for her. And if she's more than lucky, if she's truly fortunate, she has a husband who never asks, "Why are you doing this?" He just pulls on his boots and trucks out into the snowy night for yet another ream of paper and a printer cartridge.

There are some things a writer can work toward, learning to write to the best of your ability, and regarding criticism as a blessing far more valuable than any compliment, and letting the world's finest children's book agent (Jennifer Flannery) know you are out there. But there are some things only the mysterious workings of the universe can take credit for.

Like the signs posted along the way. Like the teachers who arrive so unexpectedly. Like the way my editor (Kathy Dawson) turned out to be someone who could inhale a manuscript and, on the exhale, elicit not only the parts of the story I didn't know I knew, but the very parts that helped to make this the very finest work I have ever done, and that just coincidentally were the very details that make the story whole and as near perfect as it could become.

I am forever grateful to them all.

Before Jennifer and Kathy, there were knowledgeable readers: Abby Williams Gese. Miriam, Stacy, Suzanne, Uma. Carol, Susan, Phyllis, and Stephen. Alix, Lee, Tina, Barbara, Miss Maris, Arline, and my husband, Akila. And there were my children, Nikki and Zac, strong supporters who've lived their whole lives with the Aunt Patty and the Willa Jo in me, which is no doubt how I came to know these characters so well. Thank you all for your patience and kindness.

This book is dedicated to Mama Nicky's memory.

One of my most sustaining memories of her
is that of my small children running before me.
And the way she dropped whatever she was working on,
the way she sat forward to meet them, the nearly
straight line of her as her arms opened to welcome them.

CONTENTS

1

Early Morning

Aunt Patty is fed up with me.

She told me so last night. When I got into bed, there was a sick feeling in my stomach that stayed with me through my sleep. I came out here to breathe deep of the fresh air but that sick feeling has not yet gone away.

And then Mrs. Garber ran by. Who would think somebody fifty years old would be up and running down the road before daybreak? She ran by and then she ran back and stared at me from the road, her knees all the time pumping up and down. I didn't say a word to her.

She came up to the house and rang the doorbell. I

heard the doorbell and I heard her sneakers on the flag-stone patio, *pum, pum, pum.* My stomach started to hurt.

No answer.

After a couple of minutes she rings the doorbell again. A light comes on. I see a pale yellow square in the grass, like a shadow in reverse. *Pum, pum, pum.* The front door opens. Aunt Patty's voice breaks the silence of early morning.

"Mrs. Garber, is there something wrong?"

There are whispers. A squawk from Aunt Patty, and more whispers. I wrap my arms more tightly around my knees. Pretty soon Mrs. Garber is on her way down the road again. She does not look back once.

The front door closes.

My heart feels like there is a string tied around it, with something heavy hanging from the string. I don't like it. But the sky has broken pink and is stretching pale lavender fingers toward heaven. So I make up my mind to watch those sky fingers fade to nothing, to be burned away by the sunrise.

And here it comes.

A thin rim of orange-red, so deep and strong my heart almost breaks with the fierceness of that color. Moment by moment, there is more of it to see. So hot and bright, I cannot look but at the edges. Even when I look away, look clear away to the waning edge of darkness, I can see that color in my mind's eye, feel it beating in my very blood. I breathe color.

All at once the neighborhood is waking up. A phone rings not too far away. It may even be Aunt Patty's phone. Two pickup trucks come out from the piney woods, turn off in the direction that Mrs. Garber ran. A dog barks. Next door, Mrs. Biddle puts her cat out. Squeaky spring of her back door, slam. I hear an alarm clock go off. An old-timey miner's clock that goes *Braaaaaang*.

Below, the front door opens again. "Willa Jo Dean, what do you think you're doing up there?"

I think, *Watching the sun rise.*

I came up on the roof to watch the sun rise and I just stayed, I could say.

"I know Little Sister is up there with you," Aunt Patty says, as if I was keeping it a secret. Little Sister is here because she follows me everywhere. Everyone knows that.

"Willa Jo, don't you act like you can just ignore me, now."

No one can ignore Aunt Patty, that's part of the trouble. She has that kind of voice. There isn't any hope of ignoring her.

I take off my leather sandals and place them so the heels are caught on a ridge and they won't slide down. Little Sister is already barefoot. I inch across the roof that feels like it has been sprinkled with coarse salt, liking the way the scratchy surface clutches at the fabric of my shorts, clings to my skin. I don't like getting this close to the edge, all the time knowing what I'll see. And then I do.

I look down on my aunt Patty, who is looking up, her hair in pin curls. She's short and wide, and wearing a brown terry bathrobe that is the sorriest thing. From two and a half stories up, she looks like a face on a stump.

At her first glimpse of me, Aunt Patty shifts from annoyance to outright panic, her arms lift and wave like stubby branches in the wind. "Stop right there," she screams.

I do.

I only meant to get to where I could see her anyway. I wouldn't have to get this near the edge but for the fact that she won't step off the patio in her slippers. She's afraid of getting a slug stuck on her if she steps into the wet grass.

She's right, that probably would happen, there are an awful lot of slugs in Aunt Patty's lawn. But so far as I know, nobody has yet died of getting a slug stuck on them.

And then she makes like she's in charge of roof-sitting today. "Don't you come any closer. You're likely to fall right off onto the patio and crack your head wide open."

Little Sister has been inching her way down right alongside me, and then a little bit in front of me, and now she leans forward to get a good view of Aunt Patty screeching up at us. Aunt Patty rewards her with another shrill cry.

I have a handful of Little Sister's nightgown, just in case, but she isn't going anywhere. We've run down hillsides steeper than this. It does give me a funny feeling in the pit of my stomach, though, being so close to the edge. Like this roof might roll over like a big dog and heave us into the air like fleas.

"Little Sister," Aunt Patty calls. Her tone has changed to sweet and wheedling. "Little Sister, you'll listen to reason now, won't you?"

It's no use her appealing to Little Sister, who only listens to me, anyway. Another reason, Little Sister don't talk. She used to. But not now.

2

Birds of a Feather

Little Sister hasn't said word one since Baby died. At first I tried to make her want to talk. But nearly everything I asked of her could be answered with a shake of her head or a shrug. Then I did things, like tell her I planned to make sugar cookies with refrigerator dough, and I would pretend to forget. But Little Sister didn't want sugar cookies bad enough, I guess.

So I said I needed help counting how many zucchini to pick for our dinner, or counting out how many eggs the chickens laid in one day. Little Sister would stare at me like life was too serious for me to try to trick her into doing something she didn't want to. I kept at her, though, for days on end. Finally Little Sister made up that one finger meant no, two fingers meant yes, a wagging of her flat hand meant maybe. She would hold up both hands, flashing her fingers for every ten of something so she could count up to a hundred if she had to. When she was emphatic, she would flash ten fingers, telling me "NO!" Or ten fingers twice, twenty fingers, for "YES!"

Little Sister hasn't done much of that since getting to Aunt Patty's. It makes Aunt Patty nervous. She's not mean about it, she just takes Little Sister's hands in hers and holds them and keeps talking like she never noticed a thing. Or if somebody is around, she talks louder. She pulls Little Sister's hands close and pushes them down, hoping nobody will notice.

"What are the girls doing up there?" This is Mrs. Biddle, the neighbor. As sweet an old lady as you could ever hope to meet. Bakes good cookies, the homemade kind, and she's real free with them, too.

"You can see for yourself they've climbed out onto the roof," Aunt Patty says.

She shouldn't speak to old Mrs. Biddle that way, it could hurt her feelings. But that's Aunt Patty for you. If anybody ever told her she ought to have some respect for her elders, she put it right out of her mind. Little Sister scoots back far enough that Aunt Patty can't see her anymore. Then she waves to Mrs. Biddle.

"She is the sweetest child." Mrs. Biddle sighs. She is just taken with Little Sister.

"She is the spawn of the devil," Aunt Patty says clearly, and even though only Little Sister and I were meant to hear, Mrs. Biddle hears her, too.

Little Sister's face is hidden from me by the way the curtain of her hair falls over one shoulder. "She means me, not you," I whisper to her, just in case.

As sweet as if she were offering a second helping, Mrs. Biddle says, "You don't mean that, Patty." She makes it seem that Aunt Patty isn't meant to feel bad for saying such a terrible thing, she is only being given a chance to mend her ways. Mrs. Biddle makes me smile.

But not Aunt Patty. She is still glaring up at me hard enough to make me want to pull back up to where she can't see me. Or maybe her face has frozen that way.

"Patty, now you don't mean that," Mrs. Biddle says, trying again. Mrs. Biddle probably has no idea how riled Aunt Patty can get when things don't go her way, and worse, when she gets the idea she's being criticized for it.

"I do," Aunt Patty says. "I really do. I have only had them for three weeks and they are driving me out of my only mind."

This takes me by surprise. I thought I was the only one counting the days. Well, me and Little Sister.

Down below, Aunt Patty is going on at Mrs. Biddle in that shrill voice she gets when she is real upset. "How would you like to wake up one morning to Mrs. Garber telling you your nieces are up on the roof about to jump off?" These are fighting words for Aunt Patty. Mrs. Biddle might need me to come down and put a stop to this. "And Mrs. Potts calling first thing in the morning to say there are owls roosting up on my rooftop. Very funny. How would you like that?"

Aunt Patty stamps back into the house.

Mrs. Potts. I might have known. She's such a busybody. Still, she has a fine imagination. I guess that's one good thing about her. I've enjoyed some of the silly gossipy stories she comes up with. But Mrs. Garber. To think I would come up here to jump off, now that is a stretch. Anybody with eyes should be able to see. We have been here at Aunt Patty's for three weeks now, and I have had it up to here with her. All the way up to here.

3

The Trouble with
Aunt Patty

The first thing Aunt Patty did when she got us here to Raleigh was take us shopping for new clothes. "Little outfits" was how she put it, like we were dolls. Mostly striped T-shirts and white cotton blouses was what she had in mind. And what she called camp shorts. Wide legs with narrow cuffs and lots of pockets.

Little Sister and I didn't get to say one thing about what we liked and what we didn't. That is, we couldn't say unless Aunt Patty asked because she paid for everything, and she never asked. Aunt Patty knew what she wanted us to wear.

When she was done, we looked like smaller versions of

Aunt Patty, right down to our ugly leather sandals. We came back here and she put all our other clothes into a cardboard box, and I mean everything. She left us standing in our underwear, and under orders to change that. Said much as if she suspected we'd been wearing the same underwear for a week or more. Then she shoved that box with our clothes in it onto a high shelf in a hall closet. And that was that.

"Don't you girls look cute as buttons," Aunt Patty said when we came out dressed in our new duds.

"Thank you, Aunt Patty," I said, without so much as a smile. I knew I ought to try to work up some enthusiasm but I have never in my life wanted to be cute as a button. Besides, those sandals were already rubbing a blister on my little toe.

"Don't they look like new pennies, Hob?" Aunt Patty asked.

And Uncle Hob looked up from his newspaper to say, "Like new pennies, yes, I guess they do, dumplin'."

Seemed like Aunt Patty bossed everybody, even sweet Uncle Hob. Uncle Hobart. It didn't used to be that anyone called him Hob. Mom said it was Aunt Patty who started that while they were still high school sweethearts. Pretty soon everybody was calling him Hob, like he was an elf in a fairy story or something. It didn't bother Uncle Hob. He's real sweet that way.

The sad thing is, Mom said, Aunt Patty never had motherhood to lighten her. In other words, she didn't have any children of her own. Myself, I wouldn't call it sad. I'd been her niece for one week short of thirteen years and I hadn't seen sign one that Aunt Patty was pining for children of her own. She just wanted to dress dolls.

That day we went shopping, Aunt Patty took us to this cafeteria to eat lunch. There were little hot-tables set all around and we could pick out anything in the world we wanted to eat. Fried chicken, pork chops cooked with green beans, meatballs in gravy. On a cold table, there were stacks of sandwiches on plates. Every kind of sandwich we could imagine, wrapped in clear plastic.

Little Sister and I picked out sandwiches because, as I whispered to her, they were probably cheaper. Aunt Patty had spent an awful lot of money on us in only one day. I decided tuna fish for me, peanut butter and jelly for Little Sister.

"Oh, no, don't never eat tuna outside of your own

kitchen," Aunt Patty said, the moment she saw what we were choosing. "Here, have a ham and cheese, it's safer."

Then she whispered to Little Sister, "Won't you have ham and cheese too? If you pick peanut butter and jelly, people will think we can't afford better."

Now, I understood why Aunt Patty would need to warn us about the tuna fish. I was glad she told me because I never knew it wasn't safe to eat. It was obvious there was a lot we didn't know about what was safe to eat outside our own home. But to put back peanut butter and jelly because it didn't cost enough, that was pure silliness.

I kept quiet about it, though. I know I ought to be polite to my elders. Little Sister, for her part, ate ham and cheese with mustard even though she hates mustard.

There was one good thing to come out of the day, I guess. While we were shopping, I found a chocolate shop. The way it happened, we walked by an open door with this sweet rich smell wafting on outside. I couldn't tell what kind of store it was right off. The window was full of dolls and paper flowers and books and even a little table with a tea set.

I let Aunt Patty and Little Sister go on ahead. I hung

back to stand in front of the open door. I breathed deep of that lovely smell. And looked at these glass cases like I'd seen in a bakery, all filled with trays of what looked like small brown ice cubes. I didn't have time to figure out what they were because by then Aunt Patty had noticed I was no longer right beside her and had come back to yell in my ear.

"Don't ever disappear on me like that, Willa Jo." She probably didn't mean to yell. Aunt Patty's voice just naturally gets louder when she's excited. "It's not like you've never seen a candy store before," she said.

I already knew it was best to follow Uncle Hob's example and make my voice lower and calmer so that after a while Aunt Patty will settle down. In the kind of voice I'd use in the library, I said, "This isn't any ordinary candy store, Aunt Patty."

"Well, maybe not," Aunt Patty said, eyeing the window.

"Take a whiff of that smell," I said quietly.

"I wonder if that tea set is for sale."

"Let's go in and find out," I said. The prospect of buying that tea set made all the difference. Aunt Patty loves to decorate her tabletops and she adores china. Especially figurines.

We bought the tea set and a chocolate apiece. "I guess

one piece won't hurt," Aunt Patty said. Little Sister and I shook our heads. It wouldn't hurt a bit.

Aunt Patty saved hers for Uncle Hob. "My special treat is the tea set," she said. "Besides, chocolate goes straight to my hips." Which I had to agree was not a place where Aunt Patty needed another single thing to go. I didn't say so, of course.

"That's the best chocolate I ever had," was what I did say, managing to lick my fingers before wiping them on the tissue Aunt Patty held at the ready. "Maybe we ought to get a box to take home."

"Chocolate will rot your teeth," Aunt Patty said.

"*Now* you tell me," I said, the way Mom would have if she were there. Too late, I remembered that Aunt Patty never gets Mom's jokes. Aunt Patty doesn't even laugh at Carol Burnett.

"Willa Jo, I'm going to let that pass," Aunt Patty said, her lips going all thin with disapproval, "because I know you've learned from your mother to make remarks like that."

"I'm sorry," I said. I was. There was no telling how long we'd be staying with her. It would be better all around if we were getting along with each other.

"I think we ought to try on some new shoes, don't you," Aunt Patty said. Her voice was still a little high but she was smiling. That's how I knew I was being forgiven. Naturally I didn't say I didn't want to wear those ugly sandals.

But I do hate brown leather sandals.

4

Don't Do This,
Don't Do That

There was a lot to get used to at Aunt Patty's. For instance, nobody uses the front door here. We have to go through the garage and into the kitchen. Aunt Patty was real adamant about it. One day a magazine salesman came up to the front door and she wouldn't even open it to tell him to go around. She went over to the window and knocked on it to get his attention, then pointed to the garage. He didn't get it, so she had to go through the kitchen and out the garage onto the driveway to tell him how she preferred for everybody to come into the house from the garage so her carpet wouldn't get tracked up. But she didn't buy any magazines. After all that, she wouldn't even let him come in.

The plastic runners on the carpets were all we were allowed to walk on. The plastic runner that leads to the front door was pretty much useless, of course. There were corners in some rooms that had never known the touch of a human toe, nor any other, safe to say. Aunt Patty doesn't hold with having pets.

And the radio played all the time. I don't know that Aunt Patty really listened to it. I think she was used to the noise. No matter what was going on, whether Aunt Patty was home or not, no matter if Uncle Hob was watching the news on the TV in the next room, in the kitchen on the counter Aunt Patty's radio was on. I got used to it after a while, so I didn't hear it either. Not much, anyway.

Then there were the rules. No eating in any room but the kitchen. The dining room was for show. And the rule was no butts on the bed once the bed was made up. We couldn't touch anything on the tabletops. Anyway, we weren't supposed to touch the tabletops. Fingerprints, you know. The rules were clear, but as I say, it was a lot to get used to. There were a couple of misunderstandings.

We learned right off not to use the bath powder.

"It's not that I mind you using it." Aunt Patty's voice stirred the cloud of bath powder hanging in the air.

"Did we use too much?" I asked nervously. Bath powder was an expense, I knew.

"No, no, honey." Aunt Patty's voice was shrill with being afraid she had hurt our feelings. "But I don't fluff it around so much when I use it, that's all. Not so much of it ends up on the floor and on the top of the toilet seat and such."

She was good about it, really.

Aunt Patty kept a narrow cabinet on the landing where the staircase turned the corner. There was a glass front on this cabinet and six shelves inside. Aunt Patty's Hummels were set on those shelves. Hummels being little china figurines of children carrying umbrellas on a rainy day, or bending over to pet a puppy. Like that. My favorite is a little girl on a swing.

Little Sister took a shine to those Hummels right off. Every trip up or down the stairs was an opportunity to do a fresh study of them. But she already knew about the tabletops; I never thought she'd open up that glass door. I don't even know when she did it. The first I knew of anything was when Aunt Patty was on her way downstairs and made this sound like a chicken in the mood to lay an egg. A soft kind of squawk. I looked up to see her standing before that cabinet. Her eyes were wide, but she was silent with concentration. Just like that chicken I mentioned. Then she hooked her fingers under the cuffs of her shorts and gave them a sharp little snap—and opened up her cabinet.

Little Sister was playing jacks on the carpet at the foot of the stairs. The ball wouldn't bounce, of course, so she threw it in the air instead. She couldn't catch it very often, but she always picked up a jack anyway. She never once looked up while Aunt Patty stood in front of the cabinet. Curious now, I got up to take a look.

All the Hummels had been moved around. Not just re-arranged, but rearranged so that the little boy petting a dog appeared to be in the company of the boy playing a pen-nywhistle. It looked like they were about to be joined by a boy rolling a hoop. All the figurines had been set up so that they made friendly little groups, or became families, or seemed to be trying to talk to one another. Aunt Patty lines them up like soldiers.

She started to set them back in their proper places. But after she'd moved three or four, Aunt Patty changed her mind and put them back the way Little Sister had them. She closed the cabinet and with the look of someone with an errand to run, settled herself in a chair with a magazine. If someone flipping pages that fast could be called settled.

Oh, and there were the newts.

Small reddish-brown newts lived in the woods behind Aunt Patty's house and in the woods across the road. At home, we don't have so many trees close by. If we wanted a newt, we had to drag our fingers through the mud at the edge of the pond, and if we were lucky, we might find one or two. But the first rainy day at Aunt Patty's led to a wonderful discovery.

The rain brought out newts by the hundreds. They were in the grass, on the driveway, crossing the patio. Everywhere we looked, newts were out taking a stroll, lifting their short legs like so many little wind-up toys. They were a sight to see, but at two in the afternoon, Aunt Patty has her eyes trained on her soap operas.

"Willa Jo? Willa Jo, come in here and tell me you don't think this boy's hair is bleached. Do you see those dark roots or is that my imagination? What is this world coming to, when there will not be a single soul wearing their own hair color?"

After we decided he might just have sun-streaked hair,

Aunt Patty went on to fill me in on practically every person on this soap opera. Who was married to who else first, and so on. It was fairly interesting. So neither Aunt Patty nor I paid much attention to the open and close of the back door. Even though I remember it opened and closed pretty often. It was not until the soap opera ended, and Aunt Patty offered to put out some milk and cookies, that we found Little Sister had started a collection.

"I'll have an iced tea and sit with you girls," Aunt Patty was saying. "Aah," she screamed. "Aaaaaaaaaaaaaaah!"

I ran into the kitchen to find Aunt Patty standing with both arms outstretched before her as if she might try to catch her kitchen sink if it should up and run away. Being Aunt Patty's sink, it might. It was swarming with newts, thirty or forty of them, at a guess.

Little Sister chose that moment to come in through the screened-in porch. She was wet, she'd wiped a muddy streak across her cheek, and she had a slug glued to her ankle. She looked about as happy as I had seen her in months. She stopped dead at the sight of Aunt Patty's horrified face. One hand still on the door latch, with the other hand she held two or three wriggling newts pressed against her shirtfront.

"Oh, my stars and garters," Aunt Patty moaned. "What am I going to do now?"

It was easy, really. No one had to tell Little Sister those newts would have to go. She turned right around and headed out again. I got an aluminum pie plate and put about ten newts in it to carry them back out. Of course, they started escaping the pie plate the instant I put them in, and some of them managed it before I could get out of the kitchen. But newts are easy to catch. It wasn't all that long before Aunt Patty could scrub the sink with Comet and mop the floor twice with Spic and Span.

Outside, I found an extra garbage can lid which we filled with matted leaves and water. Little Sister put some newts in this makeshift pond. But by then, I had the feeling she was doing it because it seemed to make less trouble.

5

A Tough Nut to Crack

I look out over the countryside, like I am enjoying the view. Aunt Patty has been thinking things over for three or four minutes. For three or four minutes it has been nearly peaceful out here once more.

"Your momma would shoot me if she knew what all you were doing," Aunt Patty calls up to me on the roof. She knows it isn't true. Mom won't step on a bug. I don't even look down; I stare off into the woods beyond the bungalows. "She would die of embarrassment if she knew," Aunt Patty says.

Little Sister must think this might be true, because she scoots forward suddenly to look down at Aunt Patty. Mrs.

Biddle is startled by Little Sister's quickness, one hand flies up to grip the neckline of her dress. I was startled too, so I have Little Sister's nightgown in my grasp again.

Only Aunt Patty has not noticed anything. She is not looking up, but is looking off to one side. "This child is stubborn as cement," she mutters to herself, but both Mrs. Biddle and I have heard her.

"She's not as bad as all that," Mrs. Biddle says in a voice with only the slightest quaver, considering Little Sister has given her such a scare.

"She is. She is what my very own momma would have called a tough nut to crack," Aunt Patty says. "My momma knew what she was talking about every day of her life."

And then she says, "I'm going to have to call the sheriff, I guess." She crosses her arms over her bosom. This is something she does when she has come to a decision. I have a sudden awful feeling in the pit of my stomach, like I'm about to be in big trouble. Little Sister scooches closer to me by a few more inches, close enough that the hair on our arms touches.

"There's a bad idea," Mrs. Biddle says. "He won't do anything but call the fire department."

"Well, that's who I'll call then," Aunt Patty says. Aunt

Patty's large bosom is heaving, and she is resting her fists on the mounds that serve as her hips. I wish Aunt Patty wouldn't talk to us this way. Little Sister is kind of afraid of Aunt Patty as it is. She might never climb down now.

"Do you hear me, Willa Jo?" Aunt Patty asks. Aunt Patty sounds as hard as a church pew. "I'm going to call the fire department on you. They'll come take you down like a cat out of a tree."

"If you do, I might jump," I say. At the same time I clamp my fingers around Little Sister's arm and pull back. I don't want Little Sister to believe me. But I am satisfied to see Aunt Patty's face go all smooth and calm in the way it does when she is confronted with a garden snake. Aunt Patty thinks if she pretends to be calm, she is.

She goes on like she never heard what I said. "The fire department will probably notify the authorities, and then I'll be arrested. Do you want me to get arrested, Willa Jo?"

At this, I scoot back so I cannot be seen. Not by Aunt Patty, anyway. So does Little Sister. "Willa Jo?" And after a moment, "Willa Jo, are you coming back inside?"

After another moment, she goes back into the house, her slippers hitting the bottoms of her feet. "Hob," I hear her calling. And then silence.

"I suppose you've got your reasons for doing this," Mrs. Biddle says in the gentle way she has. Mrs. Biddle nods, smiling even. "I don't suppose you girls are going to come down one minute sooner than when you are ready to," Mrs. Biddle says, and looks as if she is waiting for an answer.

It would be rude to say, "No, ma'am, I don't guess we are." The safest thing is to shake my head. So I am trying to decide whether the right answer would be a shake of the head for no, we won't, or a nod, for yes, that's right. Mrs. Biddle doesn't know what I'm thinking, though, and she goes right on to say, "You aren't doing this to be mean to your aunt Patty, are you?"

I shake my head, no, we aren't.

"Well, that's good," Mrs. Biddle says as if she is talking to very good girls. "I know it's not the same as having your mother near you. But your aunt Patty's doing the best she can." This last is said in a way that brings tears to my eyes.

Things don't feel right here. I want to open my eyes in the morning to see my very own wallpaper with the tiny blue flowers and pink rosebuds. Aunt Patty does not believe in putting up wallpaper, not even in the bathroom. She says mold grows behind it. I want the quiet of my mother's kitchen, where the only noise is the rustle of dry cereal shaken out of a box, the coffee percolating in the pot and the crackle of the newspaper as Mom turns the pages. Aunt Patty never touches a newspaper. She says the ink comes off on her fingers. And she never turns off that radio.

I want Mom to read to us for an hour before bedtime, all of us in a clump like alligators in the sun so we can all look at the pictures together. Aunt Patty is too tired after dinner to do anything but watch television. She kisses us on the forehead and tucks us into bed before it is even full dark. We want our mom. We're worried about her having to sleep all alone. We worry that she doesn't eat right, now that she doesn't have us to feed. We miss her.

I hear Aunt Patty's bossy voice, rousing Uncle Hob out of his bed. She's telling him he has to come outside to order us down. Or to plead with us, whichever he thinks will work. That sad feeling I have hardens into a mad feeling and I don't think I'll ever get down off this roof. I'll stay here till kingdom comes.

When Uncle Hob comes out, he is still in his blue-and-white-striped pajamas. I know this because I can see the legs sticking out from beneath his raincoat. Uncle Hob must not have a robe. He has probably never before needed a robe since he doesn't come out of the bedroom, most mornings, until he is dressed and ready for the day.

"There they are," Aunt Patty says and points up at us with a quick little motion of her hand before she crosses her arms again.

Uncle Hob doesn't say a word as he looks up at us. He doesn't look mad, he doesn't even look sad. He looks at us the way he looks at a crossword puzzle when he doesn't know the answer.

One of the neighbor ladies from down the street—her name is Mrs. Teasley—is walking by and stops when she sees us on the roof. She always looks like she is about to spit. She motions with one hand to Mrs. Biddle, something between a "come here" and a wave. Mrs. Biddle nods, hardly any encouragement, but Mrs. Teasley comes around the corner, along the street, up the driveway.

"Hob," Aunt Patty whines. And he puts an arm around Aunt Patty's shoulders.

There's something about Uncle Hob, a soft look in his eyes—maybe it's the glasses, but I don't think so—that makes it easy for a person to pour their heart out to him. I don't mean he always has the answer, unless it's mathematical, of course. But when Uncle Hob agrees that "That is some serious problem you have there," or maybe he chews his bottom lip and says, "It's a dilemma," you feel better, that's all. I can see that's how his arm around her shoulder works for Aunt Patty.

Mrs. Teasley walks smartly, as if she'd meant to come see Mrs. Biddle all along. As if she has not noticed us after all. Once Mrs. Teasley stands beside Mrs. Biddle, she is bold as the spots on a giraffe. She doesn't say a word but stares at us like she's sight-seeing.

"Do you see any broken ones?" Aunt Patty calls up to us in that voice she uses when we meet up with somebody in the Piggly Wiggly. I can't think what she's talking about and I stare back down at her. "Roof tiles," she says. "Any broken ones?"

A lot of things run through my mind awful fast. That Aunt Patty expects Mrs. Teasley to believe Little Sister and I are out here to check on the roof tiles. That it is only Uncle Hob's arm around her shoulders that makes her strong enough to pretend anything at all. That I had not meant to embarrass Aunt Patty. That somehow I thought I could sit up here and never be noticed at all, not by anyone. Not even by Little Sister.

When Little Sister followed me up here, I should have known that other people were bound to notice too. Not only Aunt Patty, but Mrs. Garber and anybody else who happened by. I wasn't thinking. I was just feeling. Remembering. But now things are getting out of hand.

"Willa Jo?" Aunt Patty calls.

"Not yet," I say. My voice sort of cracks and I have to clear my throat before I can go on. "I don't see any yet. But there's an awful lot of tiles."

"Well, check carefully now," Aunt Patty says. Then she looks over her shoulder. "Good morning, Mrs. Teasley. My, aren't we all the early birds?"

"Are you trying to tell me you put those girls up to climbing out onto the roof, Patty Hobson?"

"I'm not telling you a blessed thing, Mrs. Teasley," Aunt Patty says, which is bald enough to be rude. But I don't feel one bit sorry for Mrs. Teasley. Mrs. Potts probably called her to tell her to go take a look and see what Little Sister and I were up to.

Uncle Hob clears his throat and says, "Since the girls are so well occupied, I believe I might have some of those pancakes you offered me, dumplin'."

"Pancakes?" Aunt Patty says. "Oh, the pancakes. Coming right up," she says and allows Uncle Hob to take her into the house. But she sends one last nervous look in our direction.

"Where are you off to at this hour, Helen?" Mrs. Biddle says to Mrs. Teasley.

"Nowhere special. I'm taking a walk. A little hike. Good for the bones."

"Well, aren't you the one. Can't say how long it's been that I felt up to a hike," Mrs. Biddle says. "When you get back, you might stop by for a bite of berries and short-cake."

"I could do with a bite before I'm off into the wilds," Mrs. Teasley says with what could only be called a girlish giggle. I sit up straighter. It's the first suspicion I've had that Mrs. Teasley even knows how to smile. Before Mrs. Biddle turns away, she winks up at me.

Little Sister and I watch the two old ladies make their way over Mrs. Biddle's lawn, their voices high and enthu-siastic. I realize at that moment, they are friends.

6

Forbidden Friends

About a week after we'd gotten to Aunt Patty's, Little Sister and I sat on the edge of the front patio, our feet in the grass. Aunt Patty sat in a porch chair that is shaped in a circle and filled in with something stretchy like a spiderweb. She believes that chair is the best thing; she says it's elegant. But it makes her look like a turtle that's gotten flipped over on its back. Uncle Hob sat beside her in a plaid lawn chair that Aunt Patty liked to say looked cheap. Uncle Hob liked to tell her right back that he was not elegant, he was comfortable. He was not saying anything in that minute, though. He was picking out a new tune on his guitar.

Uncle Hob doesn't look like a guitar picker. He looks like somebody who reads a lot of books. It's these big glasses he wears, I guess, too big for his face. They're thick, too, like the bottoms of Coke bottles, Aunt Patty says, and she's right. But all Uncle Hob reads is the newspaper, front to back. He does the crossword puzzle so fast you'd think the answers were written on the palm of his hand. He teaches mathematics at the high school.

Across the street, nine little houses were all that was left of a bungalow colony for summer tourists. Supposedly there was a family, the Fingers, that spread itself through the more livable ones. Nine cottages, all of them needing fresh paint. Nine doors. Supposedly there were a lot of children in this family, so it worked out there was room enough for all of them this way. And enough bathrooms, too, I guess. Those bungalows, those Fingers, they were a mystery.

"You're not to associate with them," Aunt Patty had said the first day we were there. "Those children play in the dirt like mole rats."

"Mole rats," I'd said, my mind conjuring up a picture of big blind mice. "I never heard of mole rats."

"They're creatures that dig in the dirt the whole day

long," Aunt Patty said. "I saw a show about them on the educational channel."

"They're cute, but dusty," Uncle Hob said, smiling in that way he did when he teased Aunt Patty.

"They're rats. There's nothing cute about a rat," Aunt Patty said.

"They're a kind of mongoose and you've got the name twisted around somehow," Uncle Hob said.

"There's nothing cute about them," Aunt Patty said again. "Especially the oldest girl. Mrs. Biddle claims she is no more than thirteen years old. If that's so, someone should take her in hand. She's not one bit better than she ought to be."

This was something Aunt Patty had said about me once or twice, and I still didn't know that it meant anything. But I'd never lived so close to a girl anywhere near my own age. Those Fingers interested me, even if Aunt Patty hadn't made them sound too appealing.

"What are you staring at, Willa Jo?"

"I'm not staring," I said.

"Well, then, what are you looking at?" Aunt Patty said to me as she flipped pages in a magazine. So far as I could tell, this was all Aunt Patty did with magazines. She didn't stay turned to one page long enough to read it. Maybe she didn't even look at the pictures.

By the end of the first week, I'd stopped believing a lot of kids lived across the street anyway. Oh, there were lights on in the bungalows after dark, all right. But by daylight we didn't notice even one child playing out there in the grass or crying or even walking around. I watched. A couple of trucks and a little red car turned into the driveway there every so often, turned in and disappeared into the woods behind, but that was it.

"It's like looking at a row of broken teeth," Aunt Patty said to me as I continued to look across the road. The bungalows were no better and no worse than a lot of places people live but I didn't say so. It didn't matter. It wasn't enough Aunt Patty had her own opinion, she liked to have everyone else's, too.

Little Sister didn't look like she heard Aunt Patty. She stared across the street, her chin resting on her knees. Sometimes I envied Little Sister. No one expected much of her. Not only because she was only seven years old, but because she wouldn't talk. Sometimes I wished I'd thought of that.

"Quit looking over there, I told you," Aunt Patty said. "Get up and play or something."

We didn't move.

"I declare, Willa Jo," Aunt Patty said. "If I didn't understand you so well, I wouldn't understand you at all."

I had no idea what Aunt Patty meant, but I turned to look at her.

" 'Contrary,' my momma used to say I was. They were moods took me, I guess," Aunt Patty said. "Are you in a mood?"

"No," I said. I wasn't having anything Aunt Patty had.

"See there?" she said. "That's just the kind of answer I would come up with. I drove my momma crazy." She laid aside her magazine. "Maybe that's why she died so young," Aunt Patty said a little sadly.

Little Sister listened hard to every word she heard about dying and the reason why. Since she wouldn't talk, it was hard to say what kind of notions she was forming. "That isn't why," I whispered to Little Sister when her head came up.

I probably could've lived with plastic carpet runners and the radio and the sandals. But then Aunt Patty took it upon herself to pick my friends. She didn't seem to know that friends aren't something one person picks out for another, like flowers in a shop. Or that sometimes they are growing like weeds at the side of the road.

When Little Sister and I walked into town to get ice cream we stopped to sit on a log about halfway back home. The longer you walk with an ice cream in the heat, the faster it melts, until you have to put all your effort into licking. We were giving the ice cream our full attention so we didn't notice company coming until she was about right in front of us.

"Hey," she said by way of introduction. "My name is Elizabeth Fingers. People call me Liz." I recognized the name. But what Aunt Patty had failed to mention was that she was a regular string bean of a girl. Tall. Long straight black hair hanging to her hips, pale skin. She wore a straight skirt that stopped above her knees, like somebody who works in an office.

"Willa Jo." I stood up and put out my sticky hand to shake. I was not always so formal, but the moment seemed to call for it. Or her height did. She appeared to know it was disconcerting.

"I'm five foot nine, but I'm still only thirteen," she said. "I take after my uncle Beau on my momma's side, who was more'n six feet by the time he was fifteen. He's nineteen now and still growin', although he's slowed down some."

"How tall does that make him?" I couldn't resist asking.

"Six foot seven. There's nobody short in the whole family, but he's a record breaker, Uncle Beau is."

I was trying to think of something else to say since she didn't seem to mind that her family could be a matter of interest. But all that came to mind was dumb stuff like "Well, you must not have much use for step stools" or "Does everybody have to duck their heads when they go through doorways?" So I didn't say anything.

"Are you the one whose baby sister died?" she asked.

I nodded.

"I'm sorry, then," she said. "It made me cry just to hear about it. It must've broke your heart."

"This here is my other sister," I said. "We call her Little Sister. She doesn't talk."

"I know," Liz said. "Mrs. Biddle is some taken with her."

"You visit with Mrs. Biddle?"

"Everybody visits with Mrs. Biddle. You tasted her pound cake?"

I hadn't. Little Sister shook her head.

"Well, it's a mite hot for pound cake, I guess. But when the weather cools, you shouldn't miss it."

"I don't know that we'll be here that long," I said.

"Your aunt Patty signed you up for Sunday school," Liz said, as if that meant we were there for life.

I'd begun to like Liz. "Will we see you there?" Aunt Patty could hardly object to me associating with somebody at Sunday school. Why, she might never even know.

"I don't attend," Liz said. "My momma might need me to take the little one outside during the service."

I nodded. No question. There were plenty of reasons why a momma of so many children would want to keep her eldest daughter close by. The funny thing is, it squeezed my chest, thinking of it.

"It's good of your momma to spare you," Liz said. "She must miss you something fierce."

I nodded. I felt a polite response was called for. But my eyes stung with quick tears and to my horror, they started to slide down my face. I gasped and sobbed once, and breathed too deep and choked.

"Oh, hey, now, I didn't mean to make you cry," Liz said.

"I know," I said.

But I sat back down and cried anyway. So then Little Sister welled up and ran over too. In no time, Liz was sitting with her arms around both of us and she had big fat tears of sympathy on her cheeks.

"Sorry," I said when I was cried out. Neither of us had a hanky. We were about to resort to using our shirttails when Little Sister pulled several pink paper napkins out of a deep pocket of her shorts. They were from that restaurant Aunt Patty took us to. She passed them around and we all blew our noses.

"I don't know what came over me," I said.

"Don't be embarrassed by honest feelings, that's what my momma would say," Liz said.

7

After Baby Died

After Baby died, times were hard. Funerals cost a lot of money. And they make you feel tired, real tired, for weeks after. What it comes down to in the end, you stop doing everything but what you have to do.

We didn't bother about making the bed or doing the laundry. We didn't wash dishes until there wasn't one left in the cupboard. We ate from the garden, whatever picked quick, and something in a can from the pantry. Tuna fish or Vienna sausages. Eggs from our chickens. We didn't worry about breakfast, lunch or dinner. We ate whenever we were hungry.

Mom paints the pictures for greeting cards, and what she had to do was work most of the time. We didn't keep regular hours, but we'd stop whatever we were doing at sunrise or sunset. Mom would say, "Let's go out and sit on the steps and watch the sun paint the sky." We would sit together, out back or in front, leaning on each other. Even if all was not right with the world, it was in those moments at least pretty good. But Little Sister still did not speak.

One night there was a midsummer chill in the air and Mom made hot chocolate while we got into our pajamas. Then we all piled into the bed to watch the sun come up. We'd all been sleeping together since Baby died. It was less lonely that way.

Mom told us a story of Baby wanting to see some angels about some terribly important matter. She told how the angels let Baby come to them, but then they loved her so much they couldn't bear to send her back. There was more, I think, about how we would see her again someday, but not real soon, not till we were awful old, because we need each other here. Baby had the angels and we had each other.

If there was anything after that, I don't remember. I

don't even remember falling asleep. It was way later in the day when I woke up, when we all woke up to the sound of Aunt Patty's voice. "What is going on here?" she said like she'd come upon ink stains in her tablecloth. "Noreen, is there something wrong with you?"

Mom had pushed herself up on an elbow with the first remark from Aunt Patty and now she sat up completely in the bed. "Patty, what's the matter?"

"That's what I am asking you."

"We're taking a nap," Mom said in a bewildered way.

"It's the middle of the day."

"That's when people take naps."

"That's when children take naps," Aunt Patty said. "That's when grown women watch the soap operas and do their ironing. What is that smell?"

"Turpentine," Mom said, although she knew Aunt Patty knew what that smell was. "I've been painting."

"You've been painting," Aunt Patty said. It's when Aunt Patty starts to repeat words back to you that you're in the most trouble. Aunt Patty has very particular ideas about how things ought to be done.

"I want you girls to get out of those pajamas," she said. "Get some clothes on."

Little Sister and I scrambled right out of bed. We didn't even think to ask Aunt Patty where she had come from so suddenly. How she happened to come halfway across the state without calling to ask, would we be home when she got here. Not any one of us, not even Mom.

We certainly never thought of telling Aunt Patty to butt out. Aunt Patty was her big sister and Mom was used to listening to her. It was only one short step to doing whatever Aunt Patty told her to do.

What bothered me, Mom would never tell Aunt Patty how things were. She never said we were short of money. She never told Aunt Patty how tired we all were. Especially Mom. Sometimes she was so tired her paintbrush shook.

We were no sooner dressed than Aunt Patty told us to go outside and play. "What you girls need is some air," she said. "What this whole place needs is air." She began to throw the windows open all over the house.

Aunt Patty is just a force when an idea takes her this way. The best thing to do is get out of her way. Little Sister and I went out but we sat down on the steps where we could hear every word Mom and Aunt Patty said.

"I can't believe the state you have let yourself get into," Aunt Patty said. "You are skinny as a rail. Will you look at your hair? Have you combed it in a week? Have you bathed, Noreen? Even your children have lost flesh; they can't be eating properly."

There were spaces in between where Mom could have said something back if she would. But she didn't.

"This house looks like a hurricane has swept through here. It will take a month of Sundays to put it right. How would you like Social Services to come in here and take those children from you? Because they will. You don't have to be on welfare to be at the mercy of Social Services. I know. Hob has a horror story of some poor woman down on her luck for every year he has taught school."

"Oh, Patty, you don't understand," Mom said, and I was plain relieved to hear her say anything. I didn't even mind hearing her voice sound so small.

"I do," Aunt Patty said, her voice softening. "Now go on in and clean yourself up. Get all that blue paint out from under your nails. I'm going to take those girls into town and do some food shopping and when we come back, you and I are going to cook them a proper meal."

We followed Aunt Patty's instructions. It did not take a month of Sundays to put things to right—to dust and to mop and to wash every dish we owned. But when we finished at the end of the day, we were all bone tired, and even Aunt Patty could not complain when Little Sister and I fell into bed with Mom. Aunt Patty slept in my bed.

She didn't cart us off right away. Mom fell ill after the housecleaning we did the first day. The next morning she stayed in bed and slept. Then she cried. Even when she lay still and didn't make a sound, tears would leak from her eyes and trail down to her ears. She stayed in bed for a week.

When Mom was on her feet again, Aunt Patty spent two days looking for a secondhand car for Mom to get around in. Mom tried to refuse. Aunt Patty wouldn't let her. "I'm only sorry we didn't do it before this," she said in a firm voice.

Even when Aunt Patty wasn't out "kicking tires," she was weeding the garden, and fixing the drip in the shower fixture, and changing the lightbulbs that had burned out, and getting some fellow in to split wood for the winter, which she said was not all that far off.

"Firewood needs to dry out," she said when Mom said it was too early to think about firewood.

"I'll never be able to pay you back for all this, Patty," Mom said more than once.

"I hope you don't think you need to try," Aunt Patty would answer, and go on as if Mom hadn't said anything at all.

Aunt Patty put us back on regular hours, which meant Little Sister and I were in bed before it reached full dark. I would lie awake and listen to Aunt Patty and Mom talk in the night.

"I should have known," Mom said over and over. "I should have gotten to the doctor right off."

"It could have happened to any one of us," Aunt Patty would say.

And Mom would cry. So would I. I don't know why Aunt Patty kept saying that to her. Why didn't she remind Mom, like Milly did, it probably wouldn't have made a bit of difference. That's what the doctor said.

"I ought to take the girls home with me for a little while," Aunt Patty said one night.

"Oh, no, Patty, I have to hold on to my girls. I have to hold on to them hard."

"What? What do you mean?"

In low rapid words, Mom said, "I can't get over this feeling that I must have let go of Baby for just a moment. I must have let myself think of something else when I should have been holding on to her—"

"Noreen, wherever did you get such a notion," Aunt Patty said. "There isn't one thing you did that I would have done different."

"Oh, Patty," Mom said, beginning to cry again. "You would have done everything different."

On the day Aunt Patty took us away, Little Sister came as close to finding her voice as she has yet done. She held on to Mom, silent, but her lips were stretched over her teeth in a terrible grin. I thought any moment her voice would burst out of her.

"Oh, Patty, this isn't such a good idea," Mom said, clinging to me and Little Sister.

"It's a fine idea," Aunt Patty said as she pried Little Sister's fingers away from Mom. "It's the only idea. The truth is, you aren't strong enough to take care of anyone besides yourself just now. You know it. Noreen, you can't let yourself fall to the wayside again. The girls will do fine with me, won't you, Willa Jo?"

I wouldn't answer.

I looked back once as we drove away, but only for a moment. It was too hard to look at Mom standing there in the yard, looking so lost and alone.

8

Seeing the Excavation

Little Sister and I made it our business to go for ice cream the same time the day after we met Liz. Sure enough, we ran into her on the way into town.

"I work part-time down at the pharmacy," she said when I wondered if she was always here at the same time. "My aunt works the fountain. I wash the glasses for her. You going for ice cream?"

"Not especially," I said.

"Want to see our excavation?" I had no idea what she was talking about, but I preferred not to parade my ignorance. I was deciding it sounded like something medical, like the scar from a vaccination, when she added, "It isn't far."

I nodded, and Little Sister fell into step with us.

We followed Liz over what felt like hill and dale in the heat, but she called it a shortcut. After ten minutes of walking I could not have found my way back to Aunt Patty's for love nor money. Mostly this was because Liz kept to the trees. And because she didn't give a person time to get a question in sideways.

"The piney woods hereabout are riddled with holes the boys dug," she said. "Some of them are covered over with rocks or boards. They hoard things in those holes," she said. "Rusted trucks with a missing wheel. A bottle of nail polish my momma's sister, Ruby, threw away. A nice enough color on its own, but it's strange to see toenails painted dark blue. Hard to say what the boys'll ever do with it. My brothers, I mean. In one hole there's a dead bird they decided to save so they could see how long it took to get down to bones. Of course, now they've looked once and it wasn't yet, they don't really want to look again."

We ended up at the back side of the nine bungalows in a row. I realized we were across the street from Aunt Patty's. This solved some of the mystery I was not supposed to stare at. Those bungalows had a door front *and* back, and it was clear to me now that the Fingers only used the doors on the back side.

In fact, what I took to be the front side was really the back side. There were nice little porches in front of each door on the side that I'd taken to be the back side. Each porch was swept clean as a kitchen; boots and shoes were placed in a tidy row along the wall. Jackets and hats hung on hooks between the door and a window. There was a wooden box on one, like a toy box, and a rocking chair on another.

Little Sister didn't miss a thing. She pointed to whatever interested her, like the toy box, and a pair of yellow rain boots. "I see," I said to her quietly. I didn't want her to feel like she had to hide seeing anything, but I didn't want to hurt Liz's feelings, either.

Liz took us straight to a hole in the side of a rise of earth. I'm not talking about a woodchuck hole. I'm talking about a dirt hole big enough to ride a bicycle into. It was shored up around the sides with tree trunks. Cut-off tree trunks of skinny trees. And dark inside. I'd never seen anything like it in my entire life. Well, I had, but only in pictures. It looked like some old-timey gold mine, so old-timey it had sort of collapsed back into the hillside.

Liz stepped in and dropped out of sight. She was gone so fast I wasn't at all sure about following her in. But I didn't like to look afraid in front of Little Sister and I let her take my hand.

We had to sit down almost right away and slide along on our bottoms. Not because we couldn't stand, but because it ran downhill too fast to walk it. I couldn't make myself run into the darkness that way.

It didn't go on that way for long, though. At least not long enough for me to change my mind before we rounded a corner into even deeper darkness.

A light blinked on.

Little Sister and I found ourselves standing up in a dirt-walled room, shaking dust out of our shorts. There were three of those plaid lawn chairs, like Uncle Hob was partial to. One of them small enough for a five-year-old to sit in. A wooden stool made a table for a melted-down stump of candle and the up-ended flashlight.

In the spill of light, I could make out a few bent spoons scattered alongside one wall, a couple of garden trowels, a broken knife and a small red Tonka pickup truck. A short pointy shovel was propped in one corner, along with two dented metal buckets and a smaller plastic bucket with a broken handle. "You dug this out?" I asked.

"Me and my brothers, mostly," Liz said. "Neat, isn't it?"

Little Sister put out a hand and felt the dirt walls. I followed her after a moment. The walls were not so dusty-dry like the floor. Hard-packed and cold. Colder in the shallow place where they'd dug last.

"This here is my uncle Larry's shovel from the army," Liz said, picking it up. "He was in 'Nam, where everybody digs holes like this. Like woodchuck burrows, he says, tunnels that lead to room after room. My other uncle, Mike, he helped us to shore it up," she said as she rubbed her hand over another of those tree trunks. "He's done some mining and he knows about these things."

I was having a hard time picturing it. It seemed to me a hole this big had to have been there in the first place, like a cave. While she was telling me about it, I was hearing Aunt Patty's voice like an echo in my mind. Mole rats. But then something Liz said caught my attention. "Shore it up?" I said.

"It fell in on us once or twice when we first got started."

She was so matter-of-fact about it. I nodded because it seemed to be the response she was looking for.

"There's a rock here," Liz said, pointing out one wall with the shovel before she put it down. "We've come across other big ones earlier on. Uncle Mike would set a fire on them. Or under. He kept that fire going till they got red hot, then he hit them with a sledgehammer and they broke into a million pieces. This one's huge. And we're in too deep to start a fire now; there'd be too much smoke. That's why we started over again here." She ran her hand over a darker hollow on one wall.

There was a sudden rumbling in the earth all around us, like an earthquake. It looked like one, with little puffs of dust in the air like smoke. We squinted our eyes against the dust.

"That's some of 'em coming home," Liz said. She didn't look worried about a few dust motes.

By all rights, I should have been scared of a cave-in. I should have grabbed Little Sister and yanked her right out of there. But it was all so new to me I didn't even react. I waited to see. "Where've they been?" I said.

"The boys like to go to work with Daddy and Uncle Larry. All except the little one, of course."

"What kind of work?" I said, feeling like I must sound an awful lot like Aunt Patty. I had to stop asking such questions.

"Oh, they do a lot of things. Fix roofs, tar driveways, build porches. Whatever needs doing. They helped to build your aunt Patty's house."

"I'm sure she appreciates it," I said. But I looked around at the walls as I said it.

"The boys are a lot of help. They run back and forth to the truck to get what's needed, and carry drinks of water, and sweep up where it's getting messy," Liz said. She had no sooner said so than there was a scuffling noise in the tunnel.

Three boys burst in, all of them looking alike and all of them about the age of Little Sister. A younger one ran along behind them, his feet moving fast enough that he didn't have to slide down the steep part like we did. His brothers caught him before he fell over at the bottom. He wore nothing but a diaper, and he dragged a rag doll through the dirt.

"These are the twins, and this here is Isaac. He was born the year after the twins," Liz said. "And Robby is the youngest. He's three." The children in Liz's family shared the same long jawbone and high forehead, narrow slanty eyes. The young one had hair like milkweed fluff—white hair that stood up and swayed as if a breeze moved through it.

So there were only the five of them, which did not seem to be so many that Aunt Patty should feel called upon to remark on it. The introductions were barely over before the boys set to digging at that shallow hollow they'd started. They worked as a team, wordlessly. They had been doing this together for a long time and it showed. The twins chipped away at the wall with the shovel and an iron rod, letting the clods fall and break at their feet. Isaac scooped the dirt into a small plastic bucket with one hand and deposited it in a bigger metal bucket.

Robby watched this for only a moment before picking up a bent spoon to help with the digging. I could see that Little Sister was itching to get at it; her eyes shone with wanting to. If there was one thing Little Sister loved, it was dirt.

"We lug the dirt out in these buckets," Liz said. "Daddy used the dirt to make Mom a raised garden so she doesn't have to kneel to weed."

"How many of you work on it?"

"Just us kids, mostly," she said. Then whispered, "Robby's too little to accomplish much."

Maybe. But he kept up a steady pace, his little shoulder blade working like the spoon. Much of the dirt he dislodged fell right into the front of his diaper.

"And Uncle Larry helps." Liz added, "Uncle Mike, of course. But he doesn't do any digging."

Little Sister took up a kind of garden fork with a short handle. She looked at me and then Liz for permission.

"Go on, then," I said.

She picked herself a spot between Isaac and Robby and scratched away at the wall. It took her a minute or so to get the hang of it, but then she began to make real progress. The dirt fell like rain. It was only a few minutes before her toes were covered with small red mounds that were not dislodged even when she shifted her feet around.

"Might's well set a spell," Liz said, and put a hand out to offer me the best chair. The one with silver tape across the seat. It didn't even wobble when I sat down.

The other one creaked dangerously when Liz leaned back and crossed her legs the way Aunt Patty tended to do. After a moment, one of the plastic strips snapped, jarring her a bit, but she only smiled a tight little smile, no more than she would have done if she'd had to slap a mosquito.

"Are you going anywhere with it?" I asked, recalling something I'd once heard Aunt Patty say about tunneling straight through to China. I didn't figure on China, but they might have gotten to nearby Chapel Hill the way they were going.

"Not really," Liz said. "We've talked about digging up through the floor of one of the empty bungalows, but there's little enough reason for that. We can walk through the door anytime we want."

I nodded. But I liked the idea of having a tunnel under the house.

"Then we talked about digging our way across the street. But Uncle Mike says that's probably not a good idea. We'd get in a lot of trouble if the road fell through. So we're heading back through the woods with it. We'll keep going till we get tired or hit water."

"Digging might run in our family," I said. We've been coal miners for as long as anybody can remember. My daddy and both my granddaddies and their granddaddies were coal miners. And before that I had a granddaddy who was a gold miner. He got rich in California, rich enough to send my grandma back east to meet his family. Then got himself shot dead over the title to his mine, so she never went back west. But he was our family's only rich miner. Since then, every one of them has been poor as sand.

"Maybe it runs in yours," I added.

"It might," Liz said. "In the dead of one night, Uncle Larry dug himself a ditch around the edges of the village square," she added. "He said it was because he was hearing gunfire."

"Gunfire?"

"Like in the war. He believed the town was being fired upon and everyone would gather together and dig in to protect the women and children." The light was failing, so Liz reached over and gave the flashlight a shake to get it to go on a little longer.

Then she went on to say, "He believed it walking all the way into town with a shovel over his shoulder, and he believed it right up until he was about a third of the way around the square. He says he looked up then and realized that no one was shooting, that he was dreaming. But it felt so good to be digging, he said, that he just went on till he finished the job."

She paused, looking thoughtful. "So he's not crazy. Although he probably wouldn't have planted the ditch with marigolds if it hadn't been that Sheriff Batts is in the habit of showing up for the early breakfast special at Tillie's Diner on the south side of the square. Sheriff Batts insisted all that digging should be good for something. You seen those marigolds?"

I had. But when Mrs. Potts, who is Mrs. Batts' sister, told Aunt Patty to take a look at them, I had no idea what made them so interesting. I nodded as Liz went on to say, "Don't they look pretty? Uncle Larry thinks he'll put in pansies in the fall."

"Who sleeps in all the houses?" I remembered seeing the string of bungalows all lit up at night. Now that we were getting along so well, I didn't think she'd mind the question.

"My uncles each have one," she said. "My folks share one with Robby and we cook in another. My brothers share one and I have one to myself. And we rent one out to my cousin Beatrice, who works in the attorney's office in town. The others need fixing up before anyone can live in them."

I was at a loss for anything further to say, but we felt easy with each other. We sat in the faint light still coming

from the flashlight. We gazed admiringly upon the indus-
try of the younger members of our families. Little Sister
turned once and flashed me a radiant smile.

"Why won't she talk?" Liz said to me in a low voice.

"Mom thinks it must be grief. The doctor said so, anyway."

"Grief stays with a person for a long time," Liz said.

I looked at her questioningly.

"You don't worry she might lose the habit altogether, if
she goes on long enough?" Liz asked.

"Habit?"

"Talking," she said. "She gets on real well without it.
Maybe you ought to make it harder for her."

"How?"

"Pretend you don't know what she means. Or wants. Or
even what she likes," Liz said. "You look after her so well
she doesn't have to talk."

"I never thought of that," I said.

"I ought to mind my own business," Liz said, but not
like she meant it.

"No, it's all right," I said. And it was. "I know you mean
well."

"You do the way your momma decided you should. Don't listen to me. I'm too mean to my brothers by half, I know."

I hadn't noticed any meanness in Liz. She said what was on her mind, that was all. She had a point about the way I watched after Little Sister. But I wasn't sure I could do what she said to Little Sister.

Another truck rumbled in overhead, sending down a shower of dust. The flashlight died out altogether. It was dark in there, but not so dark as it had seemed when we first came in. "Getting on to supper time," Liz said. As if those words were the noon whistle, the boys put down their tools. Two of them hefted a bucket they'd filled as they trooped out. Little Sister marched right behind them.

Mrs. Fingers stepped out on her porch as we were heading back to Aunt Patty's. She was taller than Liz by some and just as slender, if you didn't count the swelling of her belly. "Hi, there," she called as she stretched and rubbed her back.

"This here is Willa Jo, Momma," Liz said. "And this is Little Sister."

"Well, isn't it nice to have some company," she said with a welcoming smile.

"This is my little sister," Liz said with a grin as she patted Mrs. Fingers' belly.

Mrs. Fingers laughed and said, "Now we don't know that yet, Liz." But she held Liz's hand flat to her belly like she liked to have it there. I ached to feel my mom's hand on mine, clinging on to me. "Would you all like something to eat? Cookies?"

"We're headed home to supper," I said. "But thank you anyway."

"You come on back anytime, you hear?"

"Yes, ma'am."

Mrs. Fingers let go of Liz's hand and rubbed her back again, which made me look at her hands instead of into her eyes. I didn't realize I was being rude till she said, "I must look a sight."

"Oh, no, ma'am," I said. "You look a fine sight."

"Aren't you the sweet one," she said. But I wasn't. It had been some time since my mom had looked like that, but I remembered it as a happy time and my heart wrapped itself around the picture of Mrs. Fingers with that baby belly. I hated to leave. But I knew Aunt Patty would be waiting.

She met us on the road as we came out of the Fingers'

driveway. "My lands, you girls look like you've been through a dust storm."

I looked at Little Sister and decided Aunt Patty was right. A fine layer of red dust rested on the shoulders of her shirt and her hair. I reached up and felt grit on the top of my head.

"Where have you been for the last two hours," Aunt Patty scolded. "I was worried to death. I even called the sheriff."

"We met Liz Finger on our way from town," I said.

"I might have known."

"We took a shortcut through the woods."

"A two-hour shortcut?"

"We talked some," I admitted.

"That was just thoughtless, Willa Jo. Don't you think I worry?" Then Aunt Patty lowered her voice to add, "Didn't I tell you to stay away from those children?"

"They don't seem so bad."

"They're let to run wild," Aunt Patty said.

9

Two Peas in a Pod

Liz came by the day after she showed us the excavation. Her little brother Robby trotted at her side, holding up his diaper. I'd seen her coming and beat it out to the driveway before she could get to the front door. I'd no sooner got out there than the front door opened. For the first time ever, maybe. But Aunt Patty didn't come out. She just stood behind the screen door.

Liz had stopped to pin Robby's diaper so it wouldn't slip. "Want to go for a walk?" she asked.

"How about we sit on the front steps," I said, because I knew Aunt Patty would have cats if I asked to go anywhere with Liz. We played jacks and let Little Sister keep an eye on Liz's brother. It was fine, if I didn't mind that Aunt Patty sort of hovered in the shadows inside the front door all afternoon. That is, it was fine till Liz's other brothers came home and wanted to play on Aunt Patty's lawn too. In all fairness, I could see why Aunt Patty thought there were so many of them. They moved fast, and three of them covered as much territory as any six boys.

"It's time you and Little Sister came on in and took your baths, Willa Jo," Aunt Patty said. "I guess all you kids ought to go on home now," she added, talking to Liz.

I felt my face go all hot, but Liz was real nice about it. She thanked Aunt Patty for her kindness in letting her brothers come to play with Little Sister. Then she rounded up her brothers and herded them toward home.

Aunt Patty didn't say another word about getting ready for bed. But I drew enough bathwater that it sloshed over the sides when Little Sister and I got in. I didn't even care. My face felt like it was wearing a mask of Aunt Patty. My mouth and my eyebrows had drawn themselves into thin straight lines that I didn't have to look into the mirror to see. We sat there till the water was cold enough to make us break out in goose bumps. Aunt Patty never said word one, not about the goose bumps and not about water on the floor. She was wearing thin straight lines too.

The next morning was a little better. Aunt Patty came out to sit on the front patio the way she never did, really, and set herself up to stay. She brought her cigarettes and matches and an ashtray and a whole armful of magazines.

Isaac brought Little Sister a present of a big june bug he'd trapped the night before. Thin red-and-white-striped string, the kind that came on boxes from the bakery, had been tied to its thorny leg like a rope around a dog's neck. The june bug could still fly, and did, it just couldn't fly away. Little Sister, and then Isaac, ran behind that june bug as it whizzed back and forth across the yard.

Liz and I looked through the magazines Aunt Patty brought out and decided who was cute and who just thought he was. Liz said all the models in the pictures are tall, like her family. She said she thought she might try getting work like that when she was older because she'd like being in rooms filled with tall people. Liz said her aunt was already talking about finding somebody to take Liz's pictures.

After a while, Aunt Patty gave us all watery lemonade

instead of the Coca-Cola I knew Liz was hoping for. Aunt Patty wouldn't let Little Sister and me have Coca-Cola. She brought out a plate of cookies, two apiece. She was none too comfortable with sweet stuff.

"I don't want your momma to say I ruined your appetite for lunch," she said. Liz and her brothers didn't need for her to hint. They each took one cookie and I could not make them take another. But they did enjoy the lemonade. They drank till the pitcher was dry. Oddly, Aunt Patty didn't mind at all. She grinned when Isaac didn't put his glass back on the tray, but handed her his empty glass and said, "Thank you, ma'am."

He and Little Sister picked a bouquet of these tiny bright pink flowers that grow no higher than new-mown grass and presented it to her while she was pretending to read her magazines. It was Isaac's idea. I thought Aunt Patty appeared to be on the verge of changing her mind about the Fingers. Anyway, I didn't mind that Aunt Patty was sitting nearby. It was better than having her hover behind the front door.

"I don't want you spending all your time with that girl," Aunt Patty said after they'd gone home for midday dinner. Said it out of nowhere, it seemed to me. I thought things

were going so well. What had Liz done wrong? As if in answer to my unasked question, Aunt Patty added, "She's too
mature for you."

"I like her."

"You're not old enough to decide what you like."

"I am, too. I know what I like and I know who I like,
too. If Mom was here . . ." But there was no reason for
Mom to be here. If we were at home—that was it—if we
were at home, Mom would like Liz just fine. Even if she
didn't, she wouldn't tell me I wasn't old enough to know
who I liked.

"We ought to call your momma today, don't you
think?" Aunt Patty asked, her voice getting higher the way
it did when she was upset. Little Sister immediately went
to her and put a hand on Aunt Patty's arm. "Yes, let's call,"
Aunt Patty said. I could see she was relieved to have the
subject of Liz dropped.

Aunt Patty dialed. Little Sister and I both reached for
the phone.

"I'll tell her who's calling," Aunt Patty said. "Then you
can talk to her. Sis? It's Patty. . . . They're fine. They're
standing right here. . . . No, they don't miss you. They have
their little friends to play with."

Little Sister's arm shot out to take the phone. So did mine. But Aunt Patty waved us down.

"Hob's fine, too. How are you doing? Are you working again?" Aunt Patty asked. "Are you keeping right hours? . . . Uh-huh. . . . Well, that sounds good. . . . Uh-huh. . . . Oh, sure, they're right here, like I said."

Little Sister reached up and snatched the receiver away from Aunt Patty. She held it as if she would have something to say, but then she just listened. Hard.

I took the phone and said, "Mom?" I sat down on the floor, pulling Little Sister with me, and held it so we could both hear. Aunt Patty stood next to us, looking down.

"Willa Jo, it's good to hear your voice," Mom said, sounding far away. Little Sister pulled the receiver up close and breathed into it.

"Little Sister is listening to you," I said loudly so that Mom would be sure to know. "I'll talk to you after."

And for two or three minutes, Little Sister sat with her ear pressed tight to the phone, her little face all aglow with hearing Mom's voice. I pried it away from her for a minute and managed to listen along with her. Mom was singing her a funny little song, but not in her usual funny little way. I hadn't heard Mom sing since Baby died. Maybe because this was so, her voice sounded rough and weak, like it didn't get enough use. It was kind of sad. I let Little Sister have the phone to herself again.

After another minute or so, she passed the receiver to me. "I'm here," I said.

"Is Little Sister all right?" Mom asked.

"She's fine," I said, because it was true. "But she misses you." Saying so made my throat feel like something was stuck there.

"I'm glad you have friends there, Willa Jo," Mom said in a breathy little voice I hardly recognized. "I miss you all—I miss you both, something fierce."

"When can we come home?"

I guess I shouldn't have come right out with it like that. I heard Mom draw in a quick breath and I saw the stricken look on Aunt Patty's face. She finally turned away from us and went to stand by the kitchen sink.

I guess Aunt Patty hoped I would tell Mom about all the new clothes, and how Aunt Patty toasted frozen waffles for our breakfast and how she and Uncle Hob were planning to take us to the drive-in movie on Friday night. Maybe even Mom hoped I would tell her those things.

But I wanted to go home more than anything. More

than I wanted Mom to be proud of me, more than I wanted not to hurt Aunt Patty's feelings, more than I wanted to play jacks with Liz. And Little Sister wanted to go home too. I didn't need to hear her say so to know it.

"Aren't you happy there, Willa Jo?" Mom said.

I knew she wanted me to say yes. But I couldn't say anything. My tongue was stuck right to the roof of my mouth.

"Are you and Aunt Patty getting along?"

I could have said, "Aunt Patty thinks because she bosses you and Uncle Hob around, she can boss us around too." I could have said, "It isn't Aunt Patty at all. I just want to come home where we can sit on the steps and sing funny sad songs. Where we can fall asleep to the rise and fall of each other's breath."

"Just remember," Mom said, as if she were feeling her way along, "two peas in a pod can rub each other wrong."

"Who are the two peas?" I said.

"Why, you and Aunt Patty, of course," Mom said with a shaky laugh. "I guess it's because you're both big sisters, you like to be the boss. Neither one of you likes to be the one being bossed."

"I don't think that's it," I said.

Mom said, "Aunt Patty will never get over it if she thinks you girls don't like it there." I had a feeling she was telling me something else. Asking me for something.

By now, the suspense had become too much for Little Sister and she got up on her knees so she could lean in and listen alongside me. I turned the receiver away from my ear a little to share it. "Little Sister is here with me," I said.

"Well, tell me what you've been doing with yourselves," Mom said with the bright and uncertain voice of someone making a fresh start.

So I told her about Liz and about the hole they'd dug, roomy as a coal miner's shaft, and about Liz's mom being so friendly and sweet, and about the june bug Isaac gave to Little Sister. "She's been running with it all morning," I said. "It's better than a dog on a leash."

"She must be going to run it to death," Mom said.

"Oh, they don't last long anyway." I didn't really know how long an old june bug goes on. But I worried that if that june bug died, Little Sister would get to thinking about Baby. "Are you painting?" I said quickly.

"Mm-hmm. I packed up some samples and drove them on up to Asheville," Mom said. "I got some extra work."

Mom was always looking for more work. But my chest

went cold at hearing of the new job. It suddenly seemed to me that Mom was finding things were easier for her if we stayed with Aunt Patty.

"We must be running up a bill," Mom said suddenly. "Put your aunt Patty back on and let me thank her for all she's done for us. You take good care of Little Sister, hear?"

"I hear."

After the phone call, Little Sister and I hardly had the energy to move. When we did, it was to avoid listening to Aunt Patty rattle on about the weather in a too-cheerful voice while sad music played on the radio. We moved to the front patio. I couldn't help thinking how different Little Sister and I would feel if Mom had told us we were going home in a day or two.

Aunt Patty opened the front door and looked out at us. "Yes, ma'am?" I said.

"Nothing," Aunt Patty said. "Just listening for signs of life." She went back inside and sat down near the door. I could hear her flipping the pages in one of her decorating magazines. I don't know what she expected to hear besides breathing.

"Did you and Liz have a falling out?" Aunt Patty asked once, through the doorway—hopefully, I thought.

"Nope."

"Where do you think she is, then?"

"Helping her mom, I guess," I said listlessly. But then I said, "She's real helpful because her mom's expecting another baby, you know. Twins, maybe."

The thought of even more Fingers was too much for Aunt Patty. She shut the front door, saying something about turning on the air.

10

Mrs. Wainwright's Daughter

We'd been at Aunt Patty's for about two weeks when we sat down to supper and Aunt Patty told us she had a surprise for us. "Mrs. Wainwright is bringing her daughter, Cynthia, over to play tomorrow afternoon."

No one said anything to this. Not me. Not Uncle Hob. Little Sister looked at me.

"This is good news," Aunt Patty said, like she had expected to see us jumping up and down for joy.

"I didn't know you were all that friendly with Lucy Wainwright," Uncle Hob said.

"I'm friendly with everyone," Aunt Patty said firmly.

"Just because we aren't bosom buddies doesn't mean we aren't friendly."

"No, of course not," Uncle Hob said.

"I don't know what I have to do to see some smiling faces around here," Aunt Patty said unhappily.

Only Uncle Hob smiled.

The next day, Little Sister and I were standing at the picture window when Mrs. Wainwright and Cynthia drove up. They got out of their car looking like they were going to church. Cynthia was not wearing camp shorts and leather sandals.

"I don't think she came to play," I said over my shoulder to Aunt Patty.

"Of course she did," Aunt Patty said, her voice getting high-pitched because she was rushing around the room, giving the toss pillows a last plump and brushing imaginary crumbs off Uncle Hob's chair.

The doorbell rang.

"They've come to the front door," I said.

"Well, of course they've come to the front door," Aunt Patty said, like it happened all the time. She gave her wide-legged shorts a little snap.

Mrs. Wainwright wore a pale green dress, the kind that has buttons all the way down the front. I noticed this because my mom loved those dresses. I couldn't see her going across the road to Milly's for iced tea in one of those dresses. I wondered suddenly if she had worn one to Asheville.

"What a pretty place you have here," Mrs. Wainwright said to Aunt Patty, without so much as a look around.

"Why, thank you," Aunt Patty said. "I'm glad to hear you think so. It's humble, but it's comfortable." There was an awkward moment when Aunt Patty expected Mrs. Wainwright to say something more, or hoped she would, I don't know. But Mrs. Wainwright didn't and Aunt Patty picked up the ball.

"You look so pretty in that dress, Cynthia. Doesn't she look pretty, Willa Jo? Have you ever seen such a dress?" Cynthia was wearing the kind of dress Mom once told me she and Aunt Patty wore when they were girls, a dress with a gathered skirt and a belt that tied in a bow at the back. They called those dresses their Sunday best. They didn't play in them. "Why don't you girls come on out to the kitchen for some refreshments?" she said, never giving me a chance to answer.

Which was just as well, considering. I was caught up in looking at Cynthia's blond ringlets, all of them growing out of a side part and held in place with barrettes. They were actually sort of horrible when I thought of how long she must have had to sit on the kitchen chair letting her mother work the hair around her finger to get them to curl just so. I wondered if I was going to end up feeling sorry for Cynthia.

We all followed her out to the kitchen, all except for Mrs. Wainwright, who veered off into the dining room. There is a little window with a sliding door in the wall between the kitchen and the dining room that usually stands open. Mrs. Wainwright looked at us through that window.

Aunt Patty put a plate of cookies on the kitchen table, allowing us two cookies apiece, just like always. She poured glasses of chocolate milk, all the time saying how much fun we were going to have.

Little Sister and I were glad to see store-bought chocolate milk. We'd been asking for it the whole time we were at Aunt Patty's and this was the first we'd seen of it. We don't get it at home either, but I figured if Aunt Patty was in the mood to spoil us, we might as well tell her what we like.

Aunt Patty talked a blue streak as she poured iced tea and cut carrot cake with orange-flavored icing that she'd brought home from the bakery. "Loaded with sugar, I know," she apologized in Mrs. Wainwright's direction. "I'll give us small pieces," she said as she cut healthy-looking wedges and put them on green plates that looked like lettuce leaves.

She invited Mrs. Wainwright to sit out on the screened porch where she said it would be cool. It would not be as cool as the dining room, where the air-conditioning was for some reason stronger than anywhere else in the house. But Aunt Patty had new porch furniture she was wanting to show off and she would sit out there even if they melted.

"Come on, Lucy," she said, like she was talking to a real sweet dog. "Make yourself right at home." Mrs. Wainwright stood a moment, like she wished she could insist on sitting in the dining room.

Meanwhile, Little Sister and I sat at the table with Cynthia, all of us looking well mannered and none too eager to start in on the cookies and milk.

So Mrs. Wainwright came around into the kitchen looking at Cynthia in that way that all mothers have, so that Cynthia would know she was to be good. Then she went out to sit on the porch. Aunt Patty was busy putting things on a tray to be carried out to the porch. The first second—and I mean the very first second—that neither Mrs. Wainwright nor Aunt Patty was looking at us, Cynthia reached over and took four cookies.

Little Sister's eyes opened wide. There were only six cookies on the plate to begin with.

"Aunt Patty," I said, although I wasn't going to tattle on Cynthia. It was the surprise of it, the words just slipped out of my mouth. But when Aunt Patty turned around, Cynthia had already hidden the cookies in the folds of her skirt.

"Nothing," I said.

"You girls be sure to have fun," she said in that singsongy voice she could have, as she lifted the tray. Her shoulders were hunched up to her ears with the effort to keep the forks from sliding around on the plates or the sprigs of mint from toppling off the edge of the iced tea glasses.

"Yes, ma'am," I said in a voice that hinted that things were not quite right with us. Mom would have known. But Aunt Patty was already talking ahead of herself, throwing her voice out to the shaded porch where Mrs. Wainwright was sitting in a throne-like wicker chair and looking like the queen of England. A big old Mack truck could have rumbled through the kitchen and Aunt Patty wouldn't have noticed.

Cynthia stuck her tongue out at me and snatched another cookie off the plate. Little Sister was on to her now, though, and she grabbed the other one, quick as a snake. We sat there staring at Cynthia across the table as Aunt Patty put down the tray and came back to slide the patio door shut to keep the air-conditioning in. Cynthia stared back.

Little Sister broke her cookie in half and slid the one half across the table to me. "You keep it, Little Sister," I said.

"I'll give you half of one of these cookies if you show me your room," Cynthia said.

"We don't need half of any cookie," I said, offended to the bottoms of my ugly brown sandals. "I can get cookies anytime I want because I live here."

"No, you don't," Cynthia said. "You're only here out of the kindness of your aunt Patty's heart."

I had nothing to say to this.

"She could send you and your dumb sister over to the

county home if she gets tired of you. That's where they put orphans."

"We aren't orphans and my sister isn't dumb."

"That's what it is if you can't speak. My mom said."

"Little Sister can talk. She just don't care to."

"And why not?"

"Because the company is none too good, that's why." I was yelling. I might have been yelling for a while, I don't know. But I finally realized Aunt Patty and Mrs. Wainwright were staring at us through the sheet glass of the patio door.

"Willa Jo," Aunt Patty called. "I think you ought to say you're sorry. Cynthia is our guest."

I looked at Aunt Patty. Mom had something she said when she put her foot down and wouldn't do something. She said, "Over my dead body." I was tempted to say it then. But I didn't.

"I'm sorry," I said with my lips, and with Aunt Patty looking on. I did not say it out loud. And I wasn't sorry.

Cynthia's mother made some little chirping sound, that's how it sounded to me. My blood was beating in my ears so I couldn't understand the words any better than that. Little Sister got up and took my hand and pulled so I'd know she wanted me to get up. I did. Cynthia got up too, all the time holding those cookies hidden in the folds of her skirt. She followed us outside.

"You girls are okay," Cynthia said as we stood outside the kitchen door in the cool of the garage. "Why don't you show me your toys?"

"We didn't bring any toys," I said. Little Sister and I walked out into the sun. Cynthia followed us.

"Then what are we supposed to do?" she said. When I didn't bother to answer she said, "I'm your guest, you'll have to come up with something to entertain me."

The thing of it was, she was right. We would never hear the end of it if we weren't nice to her. We could be old grandmommas with children racing around our knees and Aunt Patty would be there, leaning on her cane and with the frizzy ends of her gray hair bristling as she said, "I still remember how unkind you were to that little Wainwright girl; don't think I've forgotten."

"We play tag," I said. The words fell reluctantly from my tongue.

"It's too hot for that," she said. "I'll muss my dress."

After a moment, Little Sister pulled a small red ball out of one of the pockets of her shorts.

"I guess we could play jacks," I said, staring off across the street and wondering what had happened to Liz that day. "But you'll have to sit on the ground."

Cynthia flounced over to one of Aunt Patty's lawn chairs and pulled off a cushion. She dropped it on the ground and settled herself on it, spreading her skirt in a ladylike way. She ate one of the cookies while she waited.

"Go get the jacks, Little Sister," I said.

I stood away from Cynthia so she should know I wasn't warming up to her. Meanwhile, she devoured all of those cookies, flicking the crumbs off herself by shaking her skirt now and again.

"We might be friends, if you're real nice to me," Cynthia said.

I didn't answer. I might have to be nice to her, but I didn't have to be her friend.

"My mom is the president of the Ladies' Social League," she said. "Your aunt Patty isn't even a member yet."

"Maybe she doesn't want to be," I said.

"Oh, she does," Cynthia said with a little toss of her curls. "But she won't get in unless my mom likes her."

Little Sister came out with the jacks then, dropped cross-legged onto the patio and shook the jacks for the first throw. Little Sister was happy to be playing jacks.

"Is she smart enough to know the rules?" Cynthia asked as the jacks landed between them.

"Dumb means somebody doesn't speak," I said. "It doesn't necessarily mean they're stupid."

"You told me she could talk, but she doesn't. That sounds pretty stupid to me."

"Pick up the jacks, Little Sister," I said, snatching at the ones that had fallen closest to me.

"Mom," Cynthia said, opening up her mouth and letting it come out like a wail. "I'm not having a very good time."

Mrs. Wainwright looked like she knew Cynthia had not been especially nice. But when Aunt Patty closed the front door behind Cynthia and her mother, she looked like that door was closed forever.

11

Aunt Patty's Great Idea

The next day, Liz came over like always.

"Where were you yesterday?" I said.

"I saw you already had company," Liz said with a little half smile.

"I wouldn't call her good company."

"Neither would I," Liz said with a laugh and gave me a friendly push.

We looked out to where Little Sister had gone to meet Isaac at the edge of the yard. They strolled toward us, sharing Isaac's Twinkie. It seemed like a fine day was about to roll itself out before us.

"Why, Liz Fingers," Aunt Patty said, coming outside.

Liz and I looked up at Aunt Patty, who sounded less like she was greeting someone than finding a bug under a rock. But Liz said, "Good morning," as nice as you please.

"I thought you would be giving your momma a hand with the little one."

"They're napping. Isaac and I thought we'd keep company with Willa Jo and Little Sister."

"They have plenty of friends," Aunt Patty said. Lied. My face went hot. "We had a lovely visit with Mrs. Wainwright and her daughter, Cynthia, yesterday."

"That was real kind of you," Liz said. "Nobody in town will play with that snake Cynthia."

Aunt Patty managed a crooked little smile before she went back inside. Guessing that she was hovering somewhere inside the door, Liz and I only looked at each other and rolled our eyes.

Isaac pulled at Little Sister's arm. "Want to fight Charlie?"

"Who's Charlie?" I asked, wanting to keep Little Sister out of fights.

"The enemy," Isaac said, and made his arm into a gun. "Ak-ak-ak-ak-ak," he cried, spraying imaginary bullets around the yard. Little Sister looked thrilled.

Liz and I settled into watching Isaac and Little Sister play together. He told her he was in the jungle and that she was in the jungle too. Together they crawled around the shrubs at the side of the patio while Isaac rat-a-tatted a few Charlies. Little Sister did her part by holding her ears at the sound of gunfire. After a while they stopped shooting and sat quietly in the shade of a bush with long pink sweet-smelling flowers and talked.

The manner in which Isaac talked with Little Sister interested me. He never asked her a question, not even the kind that could be answered with a shake of her head. He simply told her things. For instance, he told her about a TV show he enjoyed and told her she liked it too. Little Sister didn't appear to mind going along with whatever Isaac told her.

After a time of sitting in the heat and letting the sun bring out freckles on my back, I realized they weren't talking any longer. I looked over to see they had moved out into the sun. They squatted on their heels at opposite sides of the cardboard from a Twinkies package.

They were counting the ants that swarmed over the crumb coating left from the Twinkie. Both of them were busily flicking their fingers at each other, Little Sister so sure of herself, Isaac just learning. He would sign a number to her and wait to see the agreement on her face. I was struck by the beauty of the napes of their necks as they bent over the ants. As sweet a curve as you could ever want to see. It made me miss Baby something fierce.

I swallowed noisily, thinking I might be about to cry again. I didn't want to. Liz saved me; she reached over and pinched me right below that tiny round bone in my knee and grinned. I pinched her back, right above the knuckle of her pinkie finger. She pinched my cheek and I pulled her ear, and before I knew it, we were rolling around together in the grass, shrieking with laughter.

Little Sister and Isaac fell upon us, eager to tickle and pinch and roll around. We finally lay in the grass, breathing hard as we looked up into the blue of the sky. That always makes me dizzy. It's a funny thing how I don't much notice gravity when I walk around. It is only when I lie flat in the grass that I have any sense of the earth spinning around and around, carrying me with it. It is only when I am flat to the earth that I feel the looseness of the grip in which we are held. Any one of us, at any moment, might be floating free.

A couple of days later at supper, Aunt Patty had another surprise for us. "The Baptist church has a Bible school day camp. They have two places open. You and Little Sister can attend."

Even Uncle Hob looked surprised. "I don't think it's such a good idea, what with Little Sister having decided not to talk," he said.

"Oh, she'll get over that," Aunt Patty said with a wave of her hand. "Maybe she'll get over it faster if she has so many children to talk to."

Uncle Hob didn't have an argument for that.

As evening came on and the air cooled, Little Sister decided to exercise her june bug. It was a wonder it had lasted three days. I sat there with my chin cupped in my hands, watching her run up and down and back and forth.

The light faded, and Little Sister turned the june bug over to Uncle Hob to be set free. At least that was what we figured she wanted. She showed us how her fingers were too clumsy to loosen the string.

Uncle Hob had a tiny pair of scissors in his pocketknife and he clipped the string off easy as you please without ever injuring the bug. Then he and Little Sister took it out on the porch and set it free. It flew right into the bowl of the porch light fixture and banged around on the sides. We all sat staring at the fixture till our eyes burned.

"That is one happy june bug," Uncle Hob said, blinking like a flashbulb had gone off in his face. We were all blinking.

"It's caught in there," Aunt Patty said.

"Heck, no," Uncle Hob said. "If we turn off the porch light, he'll be gone inside five minutes and probably banging around somebody else's light fixture."

"When we turn out the lights in our room at night," I said, wishing Uncle Hob would turn off the light, "we can hear june bugs banging around till we fall asleep." I didn't want to come out there the next morning and see the shadow of that june bug lying with its feet pointed up.

"You hear them banging on the walls of your room," he said. "They can get out of the light fixture, but they don't necessarily find their way out the door. This fellow, he's already outside."

Sure enough, the next morning that june bug was gone.

12

A Day at Bible School

Aunt Patty stayed "to see us off to a good start" that first morning. Most of the kids, boys and girls, seemed to know one another. Little Sister and I stood off to one side, sort of looking them over. Running and playing the way they were, no one looked unfriendly. They just looked like they didn't have any reason to want to get to know us.

"Go on," Aunt Patty called to us from the car. "Get right on in there."

I walked Little Sister over to the other side of the yard where, if nothing else, we wouldn't be able to hear Aunt Patty tell us how to be. But then this young woman stood outside all the movement and blew on a shrill whistle, blew loud enough to bend herself halfway over.

The boys who weren't already there made a dash for the ball field across the street. Aunt Patty beamed as the girls all joined hands to form a circle and sang "What a Friend I Have in Jesus." By the time the song was finished, Aunt Patty had driven off with a cheery wave that no one returned—we were holding hands.

Our teacher, whose name was Miss Pettibone, told us right off the bat that this was her first turn at being Bible school teacher, and that she would be the Bible school teacher for six whole days. She told us she was going to be our favorite. Miss Pettibone was pretty and had a voice like an angel, so I guess we all believed her.

Her assistant, Mrs. Weeds, took some of the girls off to make flowers out of pieces of egg cartons. Some of the others ran for jump ropes and Hula Hoops. The oldest girls gathered around, waiting for Miss Pettibone. But Miss Pettibone asked Little Sister and me to wait up so she could give us name tags to stick on our shirts.

Things started to go wrong right away.

Miss Pettibone didn't like that Little Sister would not tell her own name. "I'll talk for her," I said.

"That won't do," Miss Pettibone said. "You'll be in the Sunbeam Group and she'll be in, well, how old are you? Six?"

"She's nearly eight," I said. "She's small for her age."

"You'll be in the Lambs," Miss Pettibone said to Little Sister. "Do you understand? We can't be running to your sister every time you want to tell us something."

Little Sister looked at Miss Pettibone as polite as you please, but she didn't open her mouth. Miss Pettibone narrowed her eyes.

"Has she ever talked?" Miss Pettibone wanted to know.

"Yes," I said.

"Then she does talk."

"Not lately," I said. I could see this was going to turn into a big misunderstanding.

"She doesn't feel like talking, is what it is," I explained as nicely as I could, considering many of the girls were quiet and looking at me and Little Sister like we were butterflies stuck to boards with pins. "It's nothing against anybody here."

"We can't be running to you every two minutes to find out what she wants."

"She won't want anything."

So Miss Pettibone stuck Little Sister's name tag on and we began. Every time I looked over at Little Sister, she seemed to be having a fine enough time. The Lambs were the ones making flowers. They played touch tag not long after. Then they sat down to hear Mrs. Weeds read a story. I guess nobody needed Little Sister to talk as much as Miss Pettibone thought.

Our group played tag. But not until we got an old broom from the church kitchen and chased a snake off the grass. Miss Pettibone was the one who had to do the chasing. We did the running and the shrieking.

We also had to wait while Miss Pettibone pried a splinter out of the palm of the girl who carried the broom. More than one girl cried, although only the one had a splinter. This was fairly exciting, but nowhere nearly as much fun as trying to stay out of that snake's crooked path. We were all relieved to finally get around to playing the game.

When we were too hot to run around anymore, we made friendship bracelets out of braided twists of plastic. Two sisters got into a nasty fight over theirs. One sister said the other was copying her colors. It was almost as good as the snake.

We all gathered together under a tree to eat our lunches. I wasn't halfway through a sandwich before a girl named Dee Dee gave a small scream. "A tick, it's a tick on me." She began to cry.

Dee Dee had already that morning scraped her knee and had the splinter removed and had to take green Kool-Aid when the red was all gone. She cried over everything, so no one paid her any mind except Miss Pettibone, who declared it was a tick. She gave Dee Dee a look, like she thought Dee Dee might have gone and gotten this tick on purpose to ruin things.

Miss Pettibone rummaged through her purse until she found matches. "Oh, stop that sniveling," Miss Pettibone said. "You're a big girl, now act like it. Here," she said, coming up with the matches. "This is just the thing."

She lit one and blew it out, then tried to touch it to the tick on Dee Dee's leg. Dee Dee was not enthusiastic about this. "Ow, ow, ow," Dee Dee cried and jerked her leg away before Miss Pettibone got close enough to burn the tick off.

"I'm not going to hurt you," Miss Pettibone said. But Mrs. Weeds had to hold Dee Dee's leg still while this operation was performed. Mrs. Weeds looked like she might try to soothe Dee Dee's tears, but was discouraged by a mean look from Miss Pettibone. "Oh, boo hoo," Miss Pettibone said when she was finished and Dee Dee was still alive.

In all fairness, it didn't take but a moment before the tick fell right off into the grass. I don't believe for a minute that Dee Dee had the burned spot she claimed she did. She wouldn't show it to me. But while this was going on, two more girls found ticks on themselves and so the whole thing started all over. It wasn't finished before more girls found ticks.

I looked myself over, then checked Little Sister very carefully. She is the only sister I have left and I'm not letting her go to some tick bite. But even when we didn't have a tick between us, I could see Little Sister was getting that wide-eyed look she got the day Baby died. I couldn't bear to see her look that way. I wouldn't stand by helpless to do anything about it.

"They're probably falling out of this tree," I said to Miss Pettibone. I didn't sit back down and I wouldn't let Little Sister sit down either.

"I haven't seen nothing falling out of trees," Miss Pettibone said.

"Not trees, just this one," I said. "My health teacher back home explained how ticks do things. They don't have to be falling out now. They could have fallen out early this morning. Now they're waiting in the grass for some big animal to lay here in the shade."

Mrs. Weeds looked like she might be ready to leave off sitting under that tree. But she was a timid woman and she settled back when Miss Pettibone shot her another of those mean looks.

"Aren't you the little nature student," Miss Pettibone said. I know she was disappointed that things were not going well, but she had no call to be sarcastic. I might have told her so but her attention was taken up by a tick found underneath somebody's white anklet.

"Get your sandwich, Little Sister," I said. Little Sister and I went over and sat on the church steps to finish our lunch. It was hot there, and sunny, mainly because there were no shade trees. But if a tick was to get us, it would have to crawl over two feet of hot concrete to do it.

"Why don't you girls come on back here," Miss Pettibone called. It looked like the last tick had been detected and scorched off its victim. She'd had time to look around and see what everyone was doing.

I said, "No, thank you," as politely as anyone could want.

She walked over to the steps where Little Sister and I were sitting. I pretended I didn't notice her coming. She said, "You'll get sunburned unless you sit in the shade."

"Little Sister and I are used to the sun," I said. "We don't have shade tree one on our property."

Miss Pettibone narrowed her eyes at me before she went back to sit under that tree. I contemplated leaving Bible school altogether and walking back to Aunt Patty's. It wouldn't have taken any time at all if we had been wearing our tennis shoes. But we had on those ugly leather sandals that had already rubbed a fresh red spot on Little Sister's heel. So I thought we might only walk as far as the drugstore where we could ask somebody to call Aunt Patty to come get us.

This looked like the best plan and I was gathering up the waxed paper our sandwiches were wrapped in when one of the girls joined us on the steps. "She's telling stories under there now," the girl—her name was Linda—said. "It was bad enough we had to eat there, but stories? I've come to sit with you."

I decided to stay a while longer. It didn't seem right to make Linda sit there all alone.

13

The Way Things Sometimes
Work Out

The drone of storytelling went on, only now and again in-terrupted by a scream of discovery and the throes of a tick-burning. After a while there were seven of us on the steps, including Dee Dee. When another girl stood up to follow that last one, Miss Pettibone marched over to us, her face flushed an angry pink.

"I don't know why you girls insist on getting sunstroke when it is my turn to be the teacher. I'm calling your moth-ers right now to let them know how you've misbehaved."

No one said anything to this. There didn't seem to be much *to* say.

"Unless, of course, you are wise enough to mend your

ways and join the others for a game of kickball." With these words, she pointed to the empty baseball field across the street. The boys had gone off somewhere to eat their lunches and hadn't come back. She signaled to the other girls, who swarmed out from under that tree and ran for the baseball field. Miss Pettibone followed them at a more leisurely pace.

"My mom is going to be mad," Dee Dee said.

"Mine too," Linda said.

"Aunt Patty is going to be fit to be tied," I said. "Tick bites can make you awful sick."

"I mean my mom will be mad at me," Dee Dee said.

"My mom always sides with the teacher," somebody else said.

"We ought to do like she said," Linda decided. "Go on and play like nothing happened. She won't make us sit there again."

"Yeah. We might not even have had to finish eating lunch under there if Miss Priss here hadn't acted like no one could tell her what to do," Dee Dee said, looking at me. "This whole thing is all your fault."

Linda and the other girls agreed with this.

I guess Little Sister and I could've gone along and

played kickball, but I wasn't too crazy about those girls and I didn't like Miss Pettibone at all. I was counting on her making good on her threat and calling to report what bad girls we were. Aunt Patty didn't live more than ten minutes away by car.

All the same, I watched with a sick feeling in my stomach while the others marched off with that look of the saved. It's a look made up of the relief a person feels when something hasn't been as bad as they feared and of the warm feeling it gives them to be accepted back into the fold.

"You can go play if you want," I said to Little Sister. But she looked at me like the words didn't make any sense. We sat there for a while, and when the game got going, I gave Little Sister's hand a pull. But we hadn't gotten ten feet past the churchyard before Miss Pettibone hurried up alongside us.

"You girls can't go anywhere without my permission."

"Then I guess you ought to give us your permission, seeing you didn't call our aunt Patty like you said." My voice shook a little. But Miss Pettibone's mouth pocked up like she was sucking lemons.

"I made up my mind to be forgiving," she said. "I won't

tell your aunt Patty on you if you come back right now and—"

"I'm going to tell my aunt Patty," I yelled. I was suddenly so angry with her tears spurted right out of my eyes, and my mouth was so full of spit I could hardly hold it in. Even Little Sister was taken aback. "I'm going straight to the drugstore to call her and you can't stop me."

Miss Pettibone smoothed her hands over her beige slacks, like maybe her palms were damp like mine were. I was shaking all over and I think I would have buckled but for what she said next. "Mrs. Weeds seems to think you girls deserve another chance. So for her sake—"

"Mrs. Weeds, if left to herself," I said through my teeth, "would've had better sense than to make us sit under that tree once we found there were ticks in the grass." I started walking, bringing Little Sister along behind me. I was walking fast; I didn't have it in me to go slow. I couldn't believe the way I'd talked to Miss Pettibone. It seemed to me some punishment, something, must be hard on my heels.

It turned out to be Miss Pettibone. Right behind me, she was walking real fast. She would run a few steps every so often. She finally got out in front of us, keeping her back to us all the way. She never looked back to see were we there, as if she was determined to reach that drugstore before us. Or as if she intended to look like this was her idea. That was it, I realized, as we went along looking like we were following her. She wanted the people in the drugstore to think we were put to shame.

Little Sister was limping. She'd been half running to keep up. I didn't notice it right off, but the red spot on her heel had turned into a blister. So when we got to within a block of the drugstore, when we got to this corner where there is a wooden bench like it's a bus stop, except there aren't any buses in Linden City, Little Sister and I sat down to wait for Aunt Patty.

"We have matching blisters," I said to her so it would feel like this was where we ought to be. After a while, Little Sister took off her sandals and swung her feet back and forth while she waited.

Miss Pettibone walked by on her way back to the church. Her eyes were all red and puffy, and she sniffled into a fistful of Kleenex when she saw us. She hurried past us like she was afraid of getting beaten up. This seemed like strange behavior until I saw that there were two women standing outside the drugstore who were watching this whole thing. They were mostly looking at me, I think, but

I got the feeling they were more sympathetic toward pretty Miss Pettibone. After all, she was the one doing the crying. It made me real nervous about facing Aunt Patty.

It seemed like a long time before we saw Aunt Patty coming. She passed us by at first, heading for the drugstore, but she must have seen us because she made a U-turn at the corner and came on back. "Put your shoes back on, Little Sister," she said as we got into the car.

"I don't know how I'll be able to raise my head in this town. My two nieces will be known as the terrors of Stokes County." It was like the girls had guessed, she was siding with the teacher and she was mad at us. At me. It's hard to get mad at Little Sister if she won't say anything to defend herself.

I began, "She must've told you lies—"

But Aunt Patty never even paused to draw breath. I doubt she knew I'd said one word. "She didn't have to tell me you can't make it through a single day of Bible school without getting thrown out for bad behavior. You embarrassed that poor young woman, Willa Jo, do you realize that? No wonder you got thrown out. I would have thrown you out."

I was not in the mood to feel sorry for Miss Pettibone. "We didn't get thrown out, we left," I said.

"And that smart mouth of yours is exactly why," Aunt Patty said. "You sound just like your mother. If I told Noreen once, I told her a hundred times she ought not to raise a sassy child."

"It wasn't our fault. Won't you give me a chance to explain?"

"I will not. You are in the doghouse now, Willa Jo. You are to hush up until I tell you I can bear to speak to you again."

So I did. But the first thing after we got home, Little Sister scratched at something on her butt. It was a tick that had crawled up under her shorts. Aunt Patty got all flustered and didn't know what to do.

"Miss Pettibone lit matches and touched it to the ticks and made them drop off," I said. I would've felt smug if it hadn't been Little Sister that tick was attached to. "I don't think it hurt anybody," I said, so Little Sister wouldn't be scared.

"You make it sound like the woman spent the better part of an hour dropping ticks," Aunt Patty said, still sounding mad. But she was getting the box of matches from over the stove.

"She did," I said. "But she still made everybody sit in

the grass. I bet a lot of those girls still have a tick on them somewhere. Maybe I do."

It turned out I didn't. "Too ornery to attract a bloodsucker," Aunt Patty said. But she made us both strip to skin to be certain, and she wouldn't let us put those clothes back on. She hung the clothes out on the line.

"She didn't like us right from the start," I told Uncle Hob that evening. We were sitting on the shaded porch. Little Sister was running around the yard with Isaac. Only Isaac's voice could be heard.

"What was the start?" he asked.

"She wanted Little Sister to be in the Lambs, but I said I had to talk for her. She acted like Little Sister could talk if she wanted to."

"Well . . ." Aunt Patty said.

"She can't," I said.

"No, I don't suppose so," Uncle Hob said.

"Well, she could," Aunt Patty said. "It's not like her throat has been injured or anything. But she can't. Of course."

I said, "You think Little Sister is pretending she can't speak?"

"No, I don't," Aunt Patty said. "Willa Jo, that day you

all went to the fair, did Little Sister drink any of that dirty water?"

"The water wasn't dirty."

"Not so's you could see it, I know," Aunt Patty said. "But the water was bad."

"Nobody else drank it." Nobody but Baby.

We were all quiet for a few minutes. Aunt Patty swallowed so loudly her throat squeaked. I knew if I looked I would see her eyes had welled up with tears, but I wouldn't look. I was afraid she would get me started.

"Her voice was like an angel's," I said.

Aunt Patty's voice trembled when she asked, "Little Sister's?"

"Miss Pettibone's," I said.

"You mustn't take it to heart," Uncle Hob said.

"Women who don't have children . . ." Aunt Patty started, then stopped, turning a pretty shade of pink. She cleared her throat and began again. "Women who have not been with children don't know what a child goes through."

Uncle Hob rustled his newspaper like he was preparing to read.

"She didn't like us," I said, but I wasn't minding so much anymore.

"She didn't understand, that's all," Aunt Patty said. "She'd like you fine if she knew what this was all about."

"I don't think so."

"Well," Aunt Patty said, giving in after a long moment of saying nothing at all, "you might be right."

We could have gone back to Bible school the next week because Miss Pettibone lost the rest of her turn at being the teacher. Too many girls told their folks what happened and it didn't go down too well over supper.

Aunt Patty was so happy to get a call inviting us back that she didn't even mind that I said I didn't care to go. Well, she minded a little. But Uncle Hob said he didn't mind and we didn't have to go. Aunt Patty told whoever it was on the phone that we were going to be busy for the next few days.

14

The Piggly Wiggly Pickle

Things might've smoothed out after that, but for the fateful trip to the Piggly Wiggly. Little Sister was picking out breakfast cereal when a woman pushed a grocery cart around the end of the aisle and said, "Patty, is that you? I can't believe how long it's been."

"Tressa," Aunt Patty said, looking pleased. Her voice didn't even go high. "Why, you haven't changed a bit."

"I have been meaning to call you, Patty, but you know how it is. With the boys home from school, I don't have a minute."

"What are you doing all the way over here?" Aunt Patty

asked. "Don't you still live on the other side of Raleigh?"

"We've moved back," Aunt Patty's friend said. "As soon as school starts—"

"We'll get together," Aunt Patty said. "Oh, it'll be so nice to be able to have coffee with you again."

A boy of maybe fifteen came up to her and said in a deep voice, "Mom, which brand do you want?" He held up two bottles of dish detergent.

"Is this Randall?" Aunt Patty said, while her friend Tressa pointed to one bottle.

"Nope, this is Robert," Tressa said. "He's tall, like his daddy."

"Your youngest," Aunt Patty said, as Robert bobbed his head. He was shy.

"Well, not exactly," Tressa said.

A boy about Little Sister's age, maybe younger, had come from the other end of the aisle and he dropped a box into Tressa's grocery cart. "Oh, no," she said. "Not this sugary stuff. Get Corn Chex or Cheerios. And get two boxes."

He went off again.

"*That's* your youngest," Aunt Patty said almost gleefully. "You tried for that girl."

"Nope, that's Peter," Tressa said. Then she added, "Well, yes, I tried for the girl. The younger two are at home with Grandma. I have six boys, Patty. No girls."

"Six?" I could almost see Aunt Patty's thoughts written on her forehead. Six boys? Running around fast enough to look like twelve? But she recovered herself very well. "These are my nieces, Tressa. Willa Jo, say hello."

"Hello, Mrs. . . . er . . ."

"Call me Tressa," she said in a friendly way. "I've known your aunt Patty since we were girls your age. We don't have to be formal."

"Yes, ma'am," I said.

"You look enough like your aunt Patty to be her twin sister, I mean it," Tressa said. "You're the girl who took on that Pettibone creature, aren't you?"

"Oh, my lands," Aunt Patty said. "You heard about that?"

"I am filled with admiration for Willa Jo," Tressa said.

Aunt Patty didn't know what to make of this, and neither did I. "Admir—" Aunt Patty began.

"Like mother, like daughter, I guess," Tressa went on to say. "You know she's the daughter of the Mrs. Pettibone Robert had in third grade? Do you remember what a terrible year he had, that he still hadn't learned how to read? He had to repeat?"

While Tressa talked, Little Sister had taken up counting the cans of evaporated milk on the shelf beside her. She counted with quick movements of her fingers, and a thumb touched quickly to her shirt, as if this would help her remember the number. Then she went on to count the condensed milk.

"Well, the next year," Tressa was saying, "he had a new teacher, new to the district, that is. She made all the difference. He was reading by the time we moved in November. He went right into the fourth grade, where he should have been all the time."

"I had no idea," Aunt Patty said.

"And who is this pretty little thing?" Tressa said, looking at Little Sister like she was a wrapped present. Little Sister was on to counting the boxes of baking soda, thin lips moving silently to record what her flickering fingers told her.

"This is Willa Jo's little sister, JoAnn," Aunt Patty said, pulling Little Sister's hand to her side. "She's the quiet type."

Little Sister realized they were talking about her and offered up her most polite smile.

"Cat got your tongue, sweetie?" Tressa said.

"Little Sister," Aunt Patty said quickly, "why don't you get us all some donuts too? Do you know where to find them?"

Little Sister shook her head.

"Well, here's Peter," Tressa said as he came tearing around the corner again. "Peter, take JoAnn here to find some donuts, will you?"

Peter gave Little Sister a brief sizing up and said, "Come on," nicely enough. Little Sister went with a tiny smile of pleasure.

"Well, what was all that about?" Tressa said as they disappeared around the end of the aisle at a brisk walk.

"Donuts," Aunt Patty said.

"Now don't you give me that, Patty Hobson," Tressa said. "We are old friends. Doesn't that little girl hear?"

"She hears fine," Aunt Patty said in a definite tone. "I'll tell you about it some other time."

"Well, all right then," Tressa said, giving in. "Are you still on Gilbert Road?"

"No, Hob and I have built a house in a little development off—"

Just then a stack of pickle jars at the end of the aisle

crashed to the ground. Both Little Sister and her new friend Peter stood there with a pickle jar apiece and guilty expressions on their faces. The next few minutes were noisy and confused. We rushed to do what we could, but several of the jars had broken and more were rolling every which way. The smell of sweet pickle juice hung ripe in the air.

The manager of the store came around the end of the aisle with thunder on his face. Peter got scared and dropped the jar he was holding. Of course that one broke too. Peter began to cry loudly. In all fairness, he was also holding a box of a dozen donuts, and he didn't drop those. Little Sister slipped behind me, still holding her pickle jar.

"I don't know what we wanted pickles for anyway," Tressa said, looking at Peter in the way that mothers will when there are more things they will have to say later.

Aunt Patty said to the manager, "We are so sorry for the mess."

Tressa offered to pay for the broken jars, all seven of them.

But with every lady in the store looking on with interest, the manager said, "No, I don't need you to do that."

"We are truly sorry," Tressa said, and offered once more to pay for the pickles.

The manager was really pretty nice about it, considering how red his face was. But in showing Peter and Little Sister, and anyone else who might want to know, that they were forgiven, he made a big deal of speaking to them in a voice that could be heard by everyone. "This was nothing but an accident, isn't that right?" he said, and held out his hand as if to shake on it. "Could've happened to anyone."

Tressa gave Peter's elbow a nudge. Peter got the idea and shook hands with the manager. He said he was sorry in a voice that threatened more tears.

But of course Little Sister did not. She hitched up her pickle jar a notch—she wasn't about to loosen the grip she had on it—and looked at him as earnestly as anyone could want. But he didn't understand. When it became clear that the manager was waiting for another apology, Aunt Patty had little choice but to say that Little Sister didn't speak.

"I didn't realize," the manager said.

"Well, it's just for now," Aunt Patty said nervously. Every eye was on her. "We expect she'll get her voice back one of these days."

The manager was looking like Little Sister was just the saddest thing he'd ever seen. Tressa was looking at her too, as if Little Sister was sad and interesting, both. I gathered that whoever told Tressa about Bible school had not told her about Little Sister. I didn't like Tressa all at once. I didn't like the way Aunt Patty acted like she was ashamed of Little Sister. I wished she would do like Mom and just behave as if every day some child took it into her head never to speak another word.

But Aunt Patty got all flustered and rushed us out of there, only pausing to tell Tressa to be sure to call. When she didn't say another word about it all the way home, I knew she didn't want Little Sister to feel bad. But I also knew she didn't like it that Little Sister couldn't say something like Peter did and have the whole thing finish nicely.

That evening, after Little Sister had fallen asleep in the living room, Aunt Patty came out to sit on the step with me. As reluctant as ever to use the front door, she was afraid we might all get into the habit, so she came out through the garage.

There isn't any path between the garage door and the front step unless she was to walk three-quarters of the way down the driveway and come back by the S-shaped path that almost nobody uses. So Aunt Patty minced across the grass holding on to the cuffs of her shorts as if they were the folds of a skirt. Slugs.

She sat and checked her shoes. She didn't find any slugs and breathed a sigh of relief. Myself, I breathed a little sigh too. It used to be I had a little peace and quiet on the front step.

"Why do you think it is," Aunt Patty said after a few minutes of talking about this and that, "that Little Sister doesn't talk?"

"I'm not real sure," I said, never taking my eyes off the lights of the nine little houses across the street.

"Have you ever thought about it?"

"Some," I said.

Aunt Patty sat quiet for a piece, like she might have received an answer that needed some deliberation. Then she said, "Well, why do you think?"

"Aunt Patty, I don't know."

"I've never seen a child do that business with the fingers before," she said in a worried way.

"She was counting, that's all," I said. "Little Sister was counting things to keep herself occupied." I didn't feel like saying more. I had been thinking about how much Aunt Patty did not want people to know that little Sister would not speak. It made me feel tired to think about it, real tired.

"I have never seen the like," Aunt Patty said. "I wonder if we shouldn't try to snap her out of it."

Mom and I had tried plenty of times, but no matter how much Little Sister might be distracted, she never forgot not to speak. I shrugged.

"Have you tried anything?" Aunt Patty asked me.

"We've talked to her. She doesn't answer."

"Well, everybody talks to her. We ought to be able to come up with something better than that."

"Like what?" I said.

"Like things," Aunt Patty said. "To make her mad, I guess."

I turned to look at Aunt Patty.

"Like pinching her," Aunt Patty said, "or like holding her upside down by the ankles—"

"Aunt Patty!"

"Well, you know, till she says something."

"Like what?" I said, louder than I meant to.

"Well, like, 'I give up,'" Aunt Patty said in a voice suddenly gone high-pitched. "Something like that."

I looked at Aunt Patty like I was the principal of her whole life and she would have to stay after school forever if she tried such a thing.

"It was an idea," she said finally.

"It was a terrible idea," I said. "I don't think you're Mom's sister at all. I think you're Miss Pettibone's sister."

"Willa Jo," Aunt Patty said to shush me. But I wouldn't be shushed.

"It is just so like you to think you are the only one to wonder. Don't you think Mom tried to get Little Sister to talk? Don't you think I did?"

"I don't know," Aunt Patty said. "Your momma and I didn't get around to talking much about that."

"No, you were too busy making her cry."

"I never did." She looked hurt, but it was too late to pull back now.

"You said all the wrong things," I told her. "You said every wrong thing. Why couldn't you do like Milly?"

"I don't know what Milly said, Willa Jo."

"She never said anything to make Mom cry." I was nearly as angry with Aunt Patty as I had been with Miss Pettibone. But it was a confused kind of anger, mixed up with all kinds of other feelings that made my heart ache.

"I never meant to hurt your momma," Aunt Patty said. "I love her. She is my own sister, like Little Sister is yours."

Two fat tears ran down Aunt Patty's cheeks. It's just terrible to see people cry. Worse when it is my fault. It wasn't like she would really have held Little Sister up by her ankles. At least, I don't think she would.

"I didn't say the right things, though," Aunt Patty said as if the words hurt her throat. "You're right about that. I don't know the right things to say to someone who is in such pain, even if she is my sister."

"No matter what she'd done, you have to say . . ." My own words choked me. "You have to say, 'It wouldn't have made a bit of difference.' "

And I knew right then that it wouldn't. There were no right words for Aunt Patty to say. Words are not enough.

15

Second Thoughts

It's about midmorning and the roof is beginning to heat up. The sun is high and the air is kind of sticky. I wish I could get Little Sister to go back in. Her nose and cheeks are getting too pink. She pretends she hasn't heard me. I know she is feeling the sun, though. My shoulders feel tingly, and my nose burns if I scratch it.

Aunt Patty has gone back inside the house. She's gone back inside three or four times now, to dress or to do something else that needs doing. She always comes back out. I am enjoying the peace and quiet for as long as it lasts.

You'd think there wouldn't be much to do on a rooftop. But you'd be wrong. To begin with, there's the view. Green rolling hills rimmed with red clay earth, big patches of yellow buttercups and purply-pink stuff in bloom, the flash of light wherever a creek cuts across the fields.

Black-and-white cows over there and the tip-top of a red barn behind that hill.

A white church spire rising out of the valley over there where a bell will toll come twelve o'clock.

A short strip of the highway is visible between two hills and there is a never-ending stream of matchbox-sized cars that when I stare long enough begin to look like the same cars coming back again. Like they aren't really going anywhere, but are glued to a wheel that is going round and round in the distance like a Ferris wheel.

Sometimes we watch and sometimes we play. Little Sister and I devised a game of tic-tac-toe using pieces of broken roof tile somebody left beside the dormer window. The crossed lines are already there in the roof tiles that are laid all over the roof.

Or we count.

I started her on multiplication tables some time ago. I figured the numbers were so big she would get tired of counting on her fingers and speak to me. But Little Sister began to see a game in it.

She worked out new ways to give me an answer to how many of something she could count. A thousand of something is a thumb stuck out like she's hitchhiking; a hundred is a finger pointing down; and when she flashes her hands, she's holding up as many fingers as she means tens. She only ever needed the thousand sign once, when she was trying to count the gumballs in a machine. Little Sister always was sassy.

So if the number of roof tiles is 132 on this nearly square section over here, she points one finger down for the hundred, then flashes three fingers for thirty, then holds up two fingers until I've said the number she's shown me: 132. And when we add up all the sections we've counted and get 1,611, she flashes me a triumphant look. She's going to need that thousand sign again.

She jerks her thumb once for a thousand, points six fingers down for six hundred, flashes one finger and then holds one up until I say she's right. The thing is, Little Sister has the last laugh because she is fast enough that I have to stay on my toes to keep up with her. And she still hasn't had to say a word.

We counted how many green roofs there are in town, how many gray and brown, how many red, and there are two blue rooftops. You'd be surprised how most people pick the same color for a roof. There are mostly green ones, 102 that I can see.

You'd also be surprised at the amount of foot traffic Aunt Patty's dead-end street sees. Mostly bird-watchers, you'd think, since so many of them look up. A few of them have been carrying binoculars. Little Sister and I are quite the attraction.

By now, if Aunt Patty gets caught out here looking up, she acts like there's nothing at all unusual about two people sitting out on the roof all morning. She acts like she's only checking on whether we want peas or carrots with our dinner. It would be funny if it wasn't so sad.

Aunt Patty is inside when Liz comes. Liz sees me the moment she comes out from the shadow of the trees that line her driveway. She does not continue to look at me, though, as she comes across the street. There is something about that that bothers me. But when she comes to stand below and looks up at me, she has to squint into the sun.

"My momma would skin me alive if I did something like that," Liz says.

I don't know what to say to this. It's a surprise to hear her taking that scolding tone with me.

"Your aunt Patty is worried sick. She called my momma and asked her what to do."

"My aunt Patty," I say, although there is no other, "called your momma?"

"My momma told her to call your momma, but she won't do it."

"What else did your momma say?"

Liz puts on the sternest of faces. "That you are bound to come down if it rains hard enough."

For some reason, this makes me grin. And after a moment Liz grins back.

"I'm off to buy milk," she says. "I'm not to offer you any encouragement."

"You didn't," I say.

She shakes her head then and says, almost sadly, "I never thought I would feel sorry for your aunt Patty."

Little Sister and I watch her until she is out of sight. Somehow Liz has made me feel bad for Aunt Patty. She tries, I know she tries. Aunt Patty tries harder than anybody. I don't know what I hoped to accomplish by climbing out here. I guess Aunt Patty thinks I did this to drive her crazy. Maybe even Liz thinks so. But I didn't. I can't say exactly why I stayed, either. It just felt like the place I wanted to be.

One reason I'm out here, like I said, was to see the sun come up. In fact, when I went up to the attic and climbed up on a chair to push that dormer window open, I thought that was the only reason I was coming out here. It was awful quiet, not even the birds were making a sound. It was still real dark but with that hint of blue color that says the sun is coming on soon.

Huddled out here by myself, watching the sky turn from darkest blue to deep purple, I started to remember this dream I had during the night. All I could remember was something about Baby and a curtain rising.

And then Little Sister climbed out behind me. She hadn't stopped to put on shorts and a shirt like I did. She was still wearing the frilly white cotton nightgown Aunt Patty bought for her. Little Sister looked like an angel as she rose to stand on the rooftop, the breeze pulling the nightgown and her long hair off to one side the way it did. I forgot to try to remember the dream.

Little Sister crouched down and duck-waddled over to me, either because it made her stomach cramp to be up so high or because the breeze was cool, I don't know which. But she didn't act like she was cold. She sat down next to me and waited to see what would happen next, because that's the way Little Sister is. I didn't say anything, try to explain, nothing. It seemed wrong to disturb the quiet.

The air was cool and silky on my skin, and the sky kept turning more and more purple. Then came just a hint of a pink so hot it might be orange. And then it was. An orange so full of fire it looked like the edge of the world had burst into flame. Little Sister's hand crept into mine.

I let myself look for as long as I could, although Mom always warned us not to. When I looked away, I could see seven burning suns coming up all around me. But I kept needing to look back. It was like my eyes were hungry for the sight of that brilliant light. Finally, when I couldn't look straight on, I saw everything by looking off to the side. It was like watching something in a mirror.

I know it doesn't really happen this way, but it always looks as if the sun creeps up to stand teetering on the edge of the earth. I waited. It stayed there for long moments until I wondered, *Is it stuck there.* Just when I thought it, the sun made a little jump, and then it floated free.

It was in that moment that I knew joy.

I fell back to lie against the roof. Looking up that way I could see where morning overtook the last faltering edge of darkness. To look there made my stomach dip. Even my skin felt like it wanted to creep closer to the roof tiles, clinging. Little Sister leaned over me as if she might look into my eyes and see what I was looking at. Her hair slid across my face. But when she leaned away again, I didn't sit up.

I got to thinking about that dream again, not really trying hard to remember it. I can never get a dream to come back to me that way. I have to kind of tease it out, mulling over the parts I remember and trying not to make up any parts that weren't really there.

Then it did something a dream rarely does, it came back to me in one big picture. Not like a painted picture, but sort of a moving picture. Not of the whole dream, but this one piece of it. And then it was gone. Like there wasn't any more to it.

Then again, maybe that's all there ever was. Because the other thing I knew when it came back to me, I'd had this dream before—the morning Baby died.

16

A Day at the Fair

We used to be a whole family, five of us. Daddy worked at the mine from early in the morning till supper time. Mom painted cards for most of the day, and if we weren't in school, we played either outside or in the room around her. Mom didn't mind if we made some noise or ran around now and then. The only rule was: "Don't shake the table." That's how it was until sometime after our baby sister was born. Baby, that's what we all ended up calling her. She liked that.

But then the mine petered out. The owners ended up flat broke and owing money besides. Daddy looked for a job, but there wasn't enough work in the neighborhood to go around. Daddy took it real hard, but he didn't sit around the house for very long once the mine was shut down. He went off one day, looking for work—looking far and wide, he said.

I don't know that Little Sister and I missed him the way we might have. We'd been missing Mom more; she'd been so busy with Baby for the first few months. She was doing something for Baby whenever she wasn't painting, and painting if she wasn't busy with Baby.

Then Baby was big enough that Little Sister and I could watch her on a blanket on the floor while Mom painted. That was some help, and Mom could make time at the end of the day to be with us.

Although Daddy had already been gone for weeks by the time Baby could lie on the floor, it seemed like Daddy left just as Mom was coming back to us. Mostly we missed him at supper time and on Sundays. It didn't take long to get used to waiting for him to come home.

Mom missed Daddy more than we did, I guess. She hurried to the phone whenever it rang, and there were only two ways she ever looked when she answered: happy to hear Daddy's voice, or unhappy to hear that it wasn't. Happy didn't last, though. By the time she hung up with

Daddy she looked unhappy. He didn't call very often, and Mom didn't have anyone outside of us to keep company with her. Well, there was Milly, our neighbor from down the hill and across the road, and Milly counted for a lot. She made Mom laugh sometimes.

And Aunt Patty came to stay for a while, not long after Daddy left. She tried to talk Mom into moving closer to her and Uncle Hob. "Patty, I know you want to help me," Mom said.

"If only you would let me," Aunt Patty said. "You're so stubborn."

"I'm not the only one," Mom said in the voice she used for jokes. But the corners of her mouth were turned down hard.

"Noreen, you could be down the road from me—"

"That's enough, Patty," Mom said. "We can't afford to move."

"Let me help."

"I'm not a little girl anymore, Patty. You can't help me through everything."

"Not everything," Aunt Patty said. "Just this."

"We can make it on our own. We have to."

I couldn't be much help to Mom that first winter because I was still in school, days. That was also the year Little Sister started off in kindergarten, so Mom had to get her on the bus in the middle of the day. Little Sister came home with me—that was a help, I suppose. And Milly helped with Baby. But times were hard. By then Daddy wasn't calling us at all.

Mom was forced to leave Baby with Milly most of the day so she could paint. Baby and Milly didn't mind, but Mom missed Baby being nearby. A few weeks later, school was out; I could help out more with Baby. Mom said it was easier to paint with all of us back in the house.

By the time Little Sister and I were back in school, both of us for the full day, Baby was walking. She could get into the pots and pans. She opened drawers and messed up things. She didn't fuss so much to have somebody play with her. By the end of the school year, things were coming out all right for us. Better than all right.

When this little carnival came to town the first week school was out, we got into the car with Milly and went to town for the day. Baby sat up front with Mom. She didn't know what we were up to, but she was so happy about going somewhere that she kept popping up over Mom's shoulder and saying, "Boo!" Little Sister and I were giddy enough that we thought that was pretty funny. But Milly was almost more excited than we were.

"I went to this carnival when it stopped in Boone last year. They set up in the parking lot of the mall. You know how big that place is."

"It must be good, then," Mom said.

"Are there a lot of rides?" Little Sister wanted to know.

"They have all the best rides," Milly said. "Fast rides for you and Willa Jo. A pony ride and a little car ride for Baby."

"I heard they even have a double Ferris wheel for Milly and me," Mom said.

"What do you mean?" I said, never realizing Mom was teasing. "We can go on a double Ferris wheel."

"Oh no, Milly," Mom groaned. "We never get to do anything by ourselves." That's when I knew Mom was teasing, and I leaned over the car seat to pinch her upper arm. She was ready for me and caught my fingers and wouldn't let go so that I begged and laughed so much I was near to tears. We were that silly.

"That double Ferris wheel is so high we'll be able to reach out and touch heaven," Milly said.

"Really?" Little Sister would believe anything.

"Like this," Milly said, and put her arm out the open window. "We'll reach up and touch heaven."

"Hen," Baby said, her eyes shining as she reached up and touched the ceiling of the car. Mom laughed and let go of me to tickle her under the arm.

We were too small a town to have a mall or even a big enough parking lot, so the carnival was set up in Walker's washed-out field, which wasn't really in town at all. Parking was up and down the sides of the road, and by the time we got there, which was plenty early, the cars already stretched back for what Milly said was three-quarters of a mile by the meter on her car. We parked and started out walking to the carnival. It was the longest walk I'd ever taken on the edge of a road and I'd have been tempted to complain if we weren't going to the carnival.

But after a while there were things to see and the walking wasn't so bad. There were tents set up across the field for people to live in. Their laundry was hung out and flapped in the breeze like it was their own backyard. A couple of children and some dogs played in the field.

Farther on, tables were set up at the edge of the carnival for people to sell things they'd made and for others who follow the carnival to sell things we'd never find otherwise. Milly bought something in a jar to dip her eyeglasses into so they wouldn't water spot, so they wouldn't even get dirty so much. Mom bought little sweet-smelling pillows with something called lavender in them. The lavender was dark blue, not purple at all. Little Sister and I were anxious to get at the rides so Milly and Mom gave up on the shopping pretty quickly.

We moved on to the fun. There were all different kinds of rides to go on, even if the lines we waited on were long. There were little tent shows for people to look into. We made up our minds to see everything. We only skipped two tent shows that promised naked ladies.

As the day wore on, we got hot and dirty. The wind blew all the time, which made it worse somehow. There was no place to get away from the sun, unless we went back into one of the tent shows we'd already seen. We went back to see the five-legged cat, although it was a sad dead creature. It floated in a big jar of something that looked like water but wasn't. The fifth leg was a sort of extra stump growing out of one of its legs.

And we saw the stegosaurus again. That had turned out to be a picture of a stegosaurus and a big leg bone they claimed belonged to it. And we saw the gun that shot Lincoln. That is, we saw a gun like the gun that shot Lincoln. But it was hot and stuffy in the tents and we could only stay so long as somebody was showing us something. Then we were out in the sun again.

We bought straw hats to keep the sun off our faces and had to hold them on to keep them from blowing away. There was nothing we could do to keep the grass fleas off our ankles. The grass was flattened down from all the people walking out there, and the fleas were looking for something on the move to latch on to.

Baby drank up all her juice and water before half the day was out, but Mom didn't want to give her soda pop like we were drinking. "It makes her gassy," Mom said. "And then she'll get cranky."

We were on the verge of walking all the way back to the car and driving into town to get juice or water when we finally found somebody with a sausage and pepper stand who had a bottle of water he was willing to share. "It's not cold or anything," he said by way of apology. "I keep it to drown the coals, later on."

"I appreciate the kindness," Mom told him as she filled Baby's bottle.

We were all glad because it would've cut the day short. I don't think any of us would've wanted to come back to the carnival if we had to face another long walk in the midday sun. That water carried Baby the rest of the afternoon.

By the time we had seen and done everything, we were all of us hot, sticky and too tired to move, or so we claimed. But we were happy, all except for Baby, who was feeling cranky. "I think she must be getting a tooth," Mom said to Milly. "She has a little fever." Spirals of dust played around our ankles as we walked back to the car. We looked into sacks at our purchases and talked about everything we'd seen. The walk didn't seem nearly so long as it had that morning.

Mom told Little Sister and me to take a bath before we went off to bed. While we did that she washed Baby down in cool water with a little alcohol in it. I was sure we wouldn't sleep for talking about our whole day all over again; it wasn't even full dark. But I fell asleep as soon as my head hit the pillow.

Mom sat up with Baby all that night. I woke up more than once during the night to hear Baby crying and Mom crooning to her. I think I sat up once and saw Mom walking back and forth across the floor in the next room, Baby on her shoulder. I was so tired I fell back to sleep. I think I believed it was all a dream.

Because there was a dream. I dreamed Baby was lost at the carnival. Mom was looking everywhere for her and no one else even knew Baby was lost. We all came together at the last minute, Mom and Little Sister and me, in time to find Baby standing in front of one of the tent shows. We didn't run to her, which seems strange, even in a dream. She stood all alone, her little apron dress crossed over her back, the ruffles lying flat on her tiny shoulders. I could see the way her curls brushed at the nape of her neck. The tent opened like curtains it seemed, and then there was no tent; it was only curtains opening. Baby reached up with her dimpled hands and stepped inside. Just stepped inside without even looking back.

I woke from that dream sweating and with my heart beating too fast. But I saw Mom in the next room, and Baby on her shoulder. I fell back on my pillow without ever knowing for sure what was dream and what was not. I went back to sleep thinking everything must be all right.

Mom woke me so early in the morning it was still dark. She told me to run over to Milly's and tell her we had to get Baby to the doctor. Baby had been sick all night long. She rested in Mom's arms, her face tucked into Mom's neck, her breath coming fast and shallow, the way a dog pants to cool itself.

I pulled on my jeans over my shorty pajamas and ran. Mom's face looked scared, and that scared me. I remembered waking earlier in the darkness and how I fell back and went to sleep again. Now I knew I should have gotten up, I should have known something was wrong. In that minute I was sure if I had only gotten up, everything would be different. Everything would have been fine. When I left the house, the sky was only half dark—only a dark red stripe stretched across the horizon to mark the sun's rising—and I ran.

17

Until Milly Came

I banged on Milly's door till a light went on in a room above. I remember it going through my mind that I had never been upstairs in Milly's house. I didn't know which was her bedroom window. I kept on banging. All the time I was banging, even when I was thinking about Milly's bedroom window, I was aware of the sky. Instead of looking for a light, I watched a burning orange blotch be pushed aside by a hot pink glare that hurt my eyes.

"Willa Jo, is that you?" Milly said when she came to the door in her bathrobe. Milly had a lot of hair and curly, and it sprang up all over her head. She stood blinking at me, her eyes looking sort of owlish without her glasses.

"Mom says Baby is real sick, that we have to get her to the doctor." I don't know what I was suddenly hoping for, that Milly would say something that would make this go away. That she would say something that would make it something ordinary.

"It'll take me a minute to throw some clothes on," Milly said, and made it more real.

"Should I wait?" I said. I remember asking that.

"Go on back and tell her I'm coming," Milly said. "Tell your mom I'll drive right up to the door."

I ran back up the hill. Stopping once to catch my breath, I looked back over my shoulder and saw the pink had given way to a kind of charged yellow. The dark ball of the sun hove into sight. It seemed huge. Too close. I didn't want to look at it.

When I went inside, Mom was rocking Baby and the house was quiet. Baby was quiet. "You'll have to go back," Mom said to me in a whisper. She had a blanket thrown over Baby's back and it covered her face a little, like Mom meant to keep the light out of her eyes. Mom rubbed her back and rocked. "Tell Milly the baby is fine now."

"She'll be over here in a minute," I said.

"Go tell her," Mom said in a firm voice. "There's no need for her to come over."

So I did. Milly was hurrying out to the car, her curly hair swept back under a bandanna. "Mom says Baby is okay now; there's no need to take her to the doctor."

"Oh, that's good," Milly said, letting her breath out in a rush. "That she's better, I mean. I'll come up and have a look at her and see if there isn't something I can do for your mom."

"Not now," I said, because in some way I knew my mom didn't want anybody to come in and look at Baby. Maybe I even thought this would make everything okay. "Mom is going to get some sleep. She's been up all night."

"Poor thing, both of them," Milly said. "You and Little Sister come on down to my place if things are too quiet for you."

"We will," I said. But I knew that we would not leave Mom and Baby.

I wrapped myself in a blanket to ward off the morning chill and sat staring out at the day like Mom. Mom sat and rocked Baby till the mist that rises in the early morning had burned away in the heat of the sun. When Little Sister got up and wanted breakfast, Mom told me to get out the cereal and milk. She never got up to eat something herself, she didn't put Baby down to make coffee, she didn't want the newspaper. She crooned a little song in Baby's ear.

Mom rocked Baby while Little Sister and I played on the bed, dressing Little Sister's teddy bear in a Pampers and one of Baby's T-shirts. We pretended to feed the teddy bear three oatmeal cookies, but we really ate them.

When Little Sister grew tired of the teddy bear, we watched a TV show that read a book to us. Then Little Sister read a harder book to me. She'd been able to do that for a long time. She'd heard that book so many times she knew the words that went with the pictures.

And then Little Sister bounced around on the bed like the monkey she'd been reading about. Somehow she made her arms seem longer and her legs shorter. She made a soft "Ooh, ooh" sound like a monkey we'd seen on television. For an instant she didn't seem like Little Sister at all; she looked like a monkey pretending to be Little Sister. She made me laugh.

But only for a moment.

Because my laughter rang hollow in the room in a way

that laughter never had before. I couldn't say why. It bothered Little Sister too. She came to me all at once and sat on my lap and sucked her thumb. She hadn't sucked her thumb since she was real little. In all this time, Mom didn't seem to notice us at all. She didn't look at the TV, she didn't laugh with us. She didn't get out of the chair and put Baby into her bed the way she usually did.

"Does Baby want a bottle yet?" I asked Mom. "She's quiet a long time."

"She doesn't want anything," Mom said after a long moment, sounding awful tired herself. "She was up all night with the stomach cramps."

I couldn't like it, the way Mom looked, and the quiet way Baby had about her. She slept so heavily, I didn't think she'd even moved.

"Are you hungry?" I asked Mom.

"No," she said. "But you ought to make some sandwiches now, for yourself and for Little Sister."

So I did. But even in the kitchen I stood where I could look in on Mom and Baby in the rocker. Little Sister sat real quiet, looking at them. It took me a long time to make cheese sandwiches with mayonnaise, to cut them in half and put them on a plate. No one acted like they were all that hungry when I carried them in.

"You could put Baby to bed," I said. "You must be tired of sitting like that and holding her."

"No, I'm never going to be tired of holding her," Mom said. "Now go on outside and eat those sandwiches, won't you?" There was something in her voice. Something sweet and sad that made me want to hold on to her and cry. But I took Little Sister by the hand and we sat outside on the steps to eat our lunch.

Milly crossed her yard on the way to hang her laundry out. We watched her pull some pieces out of the wet twist that was mounded in her twig basket. We could hear the snap of the wet fabric when she shook them out. When she hung them they were two undershirts and a blouse, flashing brightly in the sunlight. We watched her hang her white kitchen towels with the red stripes down the sides. She struggled with two flat bedsheets that billowed all around her. The breeze was that strong.

When Milly turned around, she saw us and waved. I don't know why Little Sister and I did not wave back. Milly went back to hanging her laundry. When the last piece was up and moving in the wind, we could hear it making a sound, *buffle, buffle.* Milly picked up her basket and took it back into the house.

Like I say, I don't know why we didn't wave, but I wasn't one bit surprised when Milly came back out of the house and crossed the road and started up the rise to our house.

"Your mom inside?" she said when she got to us. Her eyes were wide, and she was breathless. All I could do was nod my head and follow her in. It was like that moment in the early hours of the morning when I stood on her porch, feeling like I'd done something wrong.

"Yoo hoo," she said, like this was any old visit. "Why, there you are," Milly said in the gentlest voice.

"Oh, Milly," Mom said.

Mom's eyes filled with tears, which made my breath catch in my throat. Little Sister ran over and put her arms around Mom and Baby. It took me by surprise is all. Milly and I were suddenly crying along with Mom, none of us making any sound, but letting the tears run down our faces. Only Little Sister didn't shed a tear.

"She was sick all night long," Mom said to Milly. "Throwing up and feverish. I thought it was something she picked up, a cold or something; you know how babies will catch every little thing. But then all of a sudden she seemed to just give up. That's when I knew it was something more. I sent Willa Jo to get you."

Milly shook her head. She was kneeling on the floor in front of Mom now.

"I sat over here where I could see her running up to your door; it was coming on light enough. The sky was so pretty, all full of cold fire, that hard burning light that makes the morning shimmer so. It was like looking at the gateway to heaven. I thought to say a prayer. I asked the angels to look down on Baby and spare her further suffering."

"Oh, honey," Milly said.

"I asked them to make her better, Milly." Mom's voice was like running water, her words coming fast and hitting all high notes. "At least I thought that's what I was asking. When the sun came up, just as the sun came up over the ridge, Baby stopped breathing. They took her, Milly. It hit me all at once, what I was asking and how it must have sounded. I should have held on to her real tight, so they would know. I must not have been holding her tight enough."

"Oh, no, Noreen," Milly cried, clinging to Mom's rocker. "They took mercy on her, that's what it must be."

"Do you believe that?" Mom said shakily. "Because if I thought it was because of something I said . . ."

"You couldn't say a wrong thing. You were praying," Milly told Mom. "I knew. I think I knew all this day. I kept asking myself how it was that you all of a sudden didn't need to go to the doctor."

"It was too late," Mom whispered.

"We're going to have to call someone now," Milly said.

"I know," Mom said. "This morning, when you were on your way over? Her little body was still so warm and sweet, I couldn't let her go."

"I don't blame you one bit," Milly said, and suddenly bent her head to Mom's knee for a moment.

Mom put a hand on Milly's head to comfort her.

"This is the hardest thing." Milly swallowed noisily two or three times. "I'll call, okay?"

"Okay," Mom said. As Milly walked over to the phone, Mom's face looked like it was breaking up. "Milly? I'm so glad you're here."

18

Seeing Baby Off
to Heaven

Milly called the doctor and asked him to meet us at the hospital. And there, he asked us what Baby had eaten. It was Mom who answered.

"I think it might have been the water," Mom said. "The girls and me, and Milly, we all drank Cokes. Baby is the only one who drank the water."

"How are the rest of you feeling?" he wanted to know. "Any fever, upset stomach?"

We all shook our heads no. He looked us over, all the same. I don't know when Little Sister stopped talking. Whether it was before we saw the doctor or sometime after. I guess most of the things we were saying to her then didn't need more of an answer than a shake of the head. And there was so much to do. Mom had to pick a little casket for Baby to rest in. Aunt Patty drove down and arrived late the next day. And in between, there were people to call, people to receive. Neighbors came by with casseroles to be put in the refrigerator and cakes under glass lids to be set in a row on the kitchen counter.

The house was so full of people and we were so sad and tired that we were either visiting or sleeping the next few days. We were simply without Baby; we didn't have time to miss her. And the single time that Mom took us to look upon her in her little bed, it was more like looking at a pretty doll—the kind no one will ever let you touch—than looking for a last time at Baby. The only way I knew for sure it was her, her name, Joy Ellen Dean, was on a little brass plate on top of her bed. Even now, the memory of it doesn't seem real.

And then, as quickly as Baby's death was upon us, the funeral was over. Baby was laid to rest, the neighbors went about their business, Aunt Patty went home. And we went so early to bed that the sun had not yet set.

I woke up in near darkness the next morning to find Mom sitting up in the rocker. She was looking out upon a mountain ridge opening up like a flower. Cinnamon-red clouds lay over the sun and washes of lavender streaked the sky like banners. "It's a beautiful sight, isn't it, Willa Jo? Like the opening of the gates of heaven."

It did look like that. It had been an arresting sight, even as I stood on Milly's porch banging on her side door. It was something to behold. Strange it wasn't ruined for us, after Baby dying at that time, I thought. I said as much to Mom.

"Maybe it's worked the other way around," she said. "Baby has made every sunrise more special in our eyes."

"Mom, have you noticed how quiet Little Sister is?" I said, because it was a moment when I could speak to Mom alone.

"It'll pass, Willa Jo," she said.

"I don't know," I said. "I've tried to draw her out. I can't get a word out of her."

"It's Little Sister's way of expressing her loss, Willa Jo. I've already mentioned it to the doctor. He says it'll pass."

It was a week or more before I happened to wake up at sunrise again. It was not much of a surprise to find Mom was awake and sitting in the rocker, looking out at the sky.

"Can you see her, Mom?" I said. Because I could see Baby. Fresh out of sleep, I could see Mom and Baby together in the rocker in my mind's eye. I had already had a few scary moments in the middle of the day when I couldn't bring Baby's face to mind and hold it there to be looked upon. And it was awful early; things can come out different before a person's full awake.

Never taking her eyes from the sunrise, Mom said, "I do, Willa Jo. I really do."

I looked out too. Light fell in straight lines through the clouds and spread like a fan. There were these wispy clouds—pink, they were, because the sun cast a rosy color over them—clouds that looked like watery drawings of two figures reaching for each other. As Mom and I watched over the next two or three minutes, the clouds touched. The smaller cloud was gathered in by the larger cloud; it seemed to fade away. I knew they were just clouds, but something made my throat clot up so bad I had to lean against Mom in the rocker.

When Mom began to paint not long after, Baby's entrance to heaven sort of took on a life of its own. That first painting was fast and kind of sloppy, like it was a thought that was going round in Mom's head and she had to slap, dash it out. Baby reaching out to two angels, who welcomed her with open arms.

But then Mom painted it again, carefully, planning for the places where it could be better. Mom painted clouds that seemed to part like curtains, so Baby could be admitted to heaven. The angels looked so real they could have blinked. Baby looked like she expected to have a real good time. Heaven was beautiful, full of light, like a hymn sung in church. We hung it on the wall over Mom's bed. To tell the truth, it about broke our hearts all over again to look at it. But it was Baby, and we couldn't put it away in a closet.

Mom painted another right after. Baby playing among the angels. And another, Baby following one of the angels around, the way Little Sister follows me. But now there were little wings sprouting on Baby's shoulder blades. Mom painted cards in the morning or the afternoon. The rest of the time, she painted Baby.

The more painting Mom did, the less she did of anything else. She didn't dust tabletops or run a dust mop or pick up books off the floor. It wasn't all that important, she said. And when it needed doing, she said, we would all do it together.

Sometimes Mom painted way into the night, only falling exhausted into bed when she worried she couldn't do more and do justice to the painting. If Mom was up painting, Little Sister and I were up watching. Our usual bedtime was suspended. It was summertime and there wasn't anyplace special we had to be.

"Why do you keep painting Baby with the angels, Mom?" I asked one night when we were by ourselves. Little Sister had earlier fallen asleep on the rug right in the middle of playing with her doll and Mom had carried her in to the bed. "Why don't you paint Baby the way we remember her?"

Mom didn't answer me right away. In fact, she took so long to say anything at all I thought maybe she hadn't heard me or hadn't wanted to. She never stopped painting the whole time, even as she finally said, "Maybe it's because I already know how Baby was here with us. I'm painting the part I don't know," she said. "I'm painting so I'll understand."

"Understand what?"

"That we don't have to be afraid for Baby, I guess. That we don't have to be afraid of joining her, too."

"Are we afraid?"

"I think maybe that's why Little Sister won't talk," Mom said quietly.

"Will the paintings make her talk?"

"Maybe someday."

I thought about this for a minute. "Why would a painting make her less afraid?"

"People have always been afraid of things they don't understand," Mom said.

"Like what things?"

"Eclipses," Mom said, after a moment's thought. "People once thought eclipses of the sun were God's judgment on something they'd done. Nowadays, we can predict the next eclipse and we aren't afraid of them."

"What else?"

"Hmmm, giant squid. Early sailors thought they were sea monsters. Well, they are, of course. But they aren't devils, or evil, or even much of a mystery anymore. Sailors don't have to fear them in the same way."

I watched in silence as Mom made soft feathers grow on Baby's little wings with a few quick flicks of her paintbrush.

"Wherever she is, do you think Baby misses us?"

"She loves us still," Mom said. "But she doesn't miss us. She knows right where to find us whenever she wants to see how things are."

"How can you be so sure?"

"I can't, Willa Jo. Not the way you want me to be sure. I can't be sure of heaven the way I can be sure of eclipses and giant squid, but someday we'll know more. And I can trust that Baby has moved on to that understanding before we have."

I sat quietly with this for a while, watching as Mom finished the work she was doing on Baby's wings. I was feeling better. I couldn't really say whether it had to do with what Mom believed. Also, I was ready to fall asleep.

Mom cleaned her brush and set it aside. "Come on," she said in a soft voice that meant things would seem more hopeful in the morning. "We're both tired and we ought to get some sleep."

"I'm glad you're painting these pictures of Baby," I said as we stretched out on the bed in the darkness on either side of Little Sister. "And not because they're the best paintings you've ever done."

"Why, then?" Mom said.

"Because it will remind us," I said. I could feel myself already sinking into sleep.

"Remind us of Baby?" she said.

"Remind us that she can always be with us."

That night I had the dream again.

When I woke I was panting like a dog. I had that feeling I had done a terrible thing, I had somehow lost Baby. Mom and Little Sister were right beside me, soundly sleeping. Mom had fallen asleep with the bed lamp on, so the room was not in darkness. Mom's first painting hung right overhead. I twisted around in the bed and let my whole self sink into the sight of angels opening their arms to Baby, to erase the scary dream-picture of Baby walking into the darkness of the tent.

19

Aunt Patty's Arrival

It was coming on sunrise when Mom finished the biggest and maybe the best picture of Baby, as a full-grown angel watching over Mom and Little Sister and me. That morning was particularly beautiful and we went outside to sit on the steps. Mom and I leaned against each other comfortably as we watched. Little Sister sat between Mom's knees. Mom ran her fingers through Little Sister's hair.

The sky was cloudy as the sun was rising over the ridge. The clouds covering the edge of the sun looked like they were on fire; they burned like hot coals. The clouds above were bathed in a heavenly glow. They shone soft and golden and were shot through with a glorious light. And suddenly

I saw it as more than a sunrise, however beautiful it might be. I saw it as Baby's new home. I saw it, I suddenly thought, the way Mom had been seeing it all along.

"All these pictures you been painting, Mom," I said. "They're really true? I mean, do you think Baby's with angels now?"

"I do," Mom said. "I really do."

"So you think it's like you painted?" I said, swallowing down a kind of pain in my chest and in my throat. But I wasn't unhappy. Just uncertain, in some way. Hoping that it could be true, and yet afraid that I would never find my way, all the way, to this belief. "That Baby will grow up to be an angel herself?"

"I think they've taken her in," Mom said. "I believe that Baby rests in the arms of the angels. But I've painted it the way I think of it. Being something like we have here on earth. It may be altogether different. It may be sweeter than we can imagine."

I nodded. Still I couldn't bring myself to believe as wholeheartedly as Mom did. All I could allow, I was relieved that Mom didn't feel Baby was all alone. Baby would've hated that.

Mom sighed as the sky settled into full morning. She

was pale and weary-looking. Milly had come over the night before and scolded her for letting herself get so thin and tried to tempt her with blueberry coffee cake.

"I picked these berries myself," she said. "Why don't you and the girls come picking with me tomorrow?"

"We might," Mom said. That was what she always said, but the paint always drew her in. Away. Mom painted, and hardly slept, and didn't eat, and sometimes forgot that we needed to eat. She didn't bother with so much else that I began to be angry with her, the way I was in the few months right after Baby was born. I don't know for sure about Little Sister, but I always felt like I was waiting, waiting for Mom to come back to us.

So I knew Milly was right to scold Mom. I just didn't expect things to change. "I'm tired," I said.

"I think we should go back inside and get some sleep," Mom said. "You girls have been up all night. Even Little Sister."

Little Sister regarded this as praise and grinned. Most nights we stayed up, Little Sister would fall asleep on the couch after hours of pinching herself to keep awake. But this time she'd made it. She'd made it all the way to sunrise. She hated to fall asleep without Mom and me.

When Aunt Patty arrived later that day, it was some relief to me. I expected she would know what to do for Mom. I expected she could make a difference. This expectation was not one I could share with Mom or Little Sister. Or Aunt Patty. Her forward manner made it hard to share such hopes with her.

I became her secret accomplice as we went from the first necessary cleanup to the beating of rugs and airing of bedstuff and finally to cleaning out the closets. Mom slept through much of this. I made it my business to be on my feet if Aunt Patty was on hers. I was her secret cheering section when Aunt Patty insisted that Mom eat everything she put on Mom's plate. I even went cheerfully—if also genuinely tired enough to go—off to bed as dusk fell. At first.

But when Mom could not be shaped up so easily as the house or the garden, I began to lose faith in Aunt Patty's methods. She would not stay forever, and when she went, I was afraid we would go back to our slipshod ways. When I heard Aunt Patty say, "Maybe I should take the girls with me," I felt like a traitor. Not just because I felt that Aunt Patty was taking too much upon herself, but because in that secret place in my heart, I wanted to go.

20

Uncle Hob

It gets pretty hot on the roof along about the middle of the day. Little Sister doesn't complain. And I'm not yet of a mind to go back inside. I'm wondering if I shouldn't get Little Sister out of the sun over there next to the chimney, although the chimney is some higher than we are now. Steeper too, that section of the roof. I'm still wondering when Uncle Hob pokes his head out the dormer window.

"Say," he says. "You girls look like you could use a drink of water. And maybe a cheese sandwich."

"We might," I say. It never occurred to me to ask for such a thing. I figured we're in enough trouble, we might as well think of ourselves as sent to our rooms without supper.

"You don't mind if I come out and keep you company, I hope," Uncle Hob says as he passes me a quart-size mason jar filled with chilled water. I notice he is wearing a tie. This makes me notice that he is wearing a white shirt, his Sunday-go-to-meeting shirt. Most days he likes a plaid shirt, which doesn't need a tie.

"Little Sister," he says, "can you take this umbrella from me?"

She does.

"Hold it there," Uncle Hob says. "Don't let it slide off the roof."

He sets a picnic basket out on the roof and climbs out.

He does not stand up, but kind of squats in the little patch of shade beside the window. I see he is altogether dressed for church in his blue pants and best shoes.

"Why are you all dressed up, Uncle Hob?"

He pushes his glasses back up on his nose. "Well, now, I always dress up for special occasions."

He reaches back inside for his guitar. But he doesn't bring the guitar out on the roof because the sun isn't good for the strings. He props it in the window. Now he stops and takes off his black leather shoes and peels off his black nylon socks. His feet are pasty white under those socks, and his toenails are so clean even Aunt Patty wouldn't find fault. Then he scooches over to sit beside us, whispering, "Ooh, ouch, hot, ooh."

Little Sister and I move aside and make room for him. It is just slightly cooler in the spot where we have been sitting. "Like sitting on a tablecloth where someone's left the iron for too long," he says. "How are you girls standing it?"

Little Sister shrugs. I say, "We're used to it by now, I guess. It doesn't seem all that hot anymore."

Uncle Hob takes the umbrella from Little Sister and puts it behind him so it can't roll away. Then he fills cups from the picnic basket with cold water. While we drink our fill he is getting out sandwiches that are wrapped in paper napkins. All of this without saying one word. I guess I should be wondering if this is a trick of some kind. Like, if Uncle Hob is trying to get us to come inside, he figures to do it by feeding us and softening us up some. But all that happens is we eat and drink and he holds that big black umbrella over our heads.

"It's mighty hot up here," he says. "Don't reckon I ever gave much thought to sunbathing, but if'n I did, this would be the place to do it."

"Guess so," I say. "Had three brand-new freckles break

out on my left foot since morning." Little Sister immediately holds out her left foot to be compared.

Then I tell him how well Little Sister is coming along with her multiplication tables and how many green roofs we counted and all. And he points out the business district and says which rooftops are the drugstore and the dime store and the movie theater. Any rooftop you point out, Uncle Hob knows what store it is on top of. This, he says, is because he used to work as a roofer when school let out in summer.

"Are you too old to do that now?" I say. I used to think he was older than he is because of the glasses he wears. But now I'm older and I realize that not all grown-ups are old. It just seems that way because they're tall.

"Oh, no," he says, like he's surprised at the thought. Right away I'm worried I've said something wrong.

"What I mean is," I say, "why'd you quit?"

"Your aunt Patty got too nervous about me working on rooftops all day long. That's when I took to painting houses."

"I don't remember you painting houses," I say.

"Well, I don't anymore. Patty got to worrying about whether I'd fall off of the ladder."

"That Aunt Patty is a powerful worrier," I say. Which reminds me that I haven't seen her out here for a while. I'm almost missing her.

That's a joke, that last part about missing her, the kind of joke Aunt Patty has very little appreciation for. None, to be exact. Since there isn't much joking in Aunt Patty's house, I don't even know whether Uncle Hob enjoys a joke now and again. So all I say is, "Where do you think she is?"

He tells us not to worry overmuch about Aunt Patty. "She isn't crying anymore," he says.

"Aunt Patty cried?"

"Only for a while," Uncle Hob says. "Then she took two aspirins and laid down with a cold cloth on her head. She's sleeping now."

This doesn't make me feel any better. "I guess she's afraid we'll fall off the roof," I say.

"She was afraid of that at first," Uncle Hob says. "But when you didn't fall off and you didn't fall off, she got used to the idea that you could sit out here without falling off."

"Then why did she cry?"

"Why, her feelings are hurt, Willa Jo." Uncle Hob looks as if he is surprised I haven't thought of this. Fact is, I haven't. He gives a deep sigh, the way some men draw on a pipe. In fast, out slow. Then he says, "Plus she's afraid your mother will find out and accuse her of some kind of neglect."

"We'd tell Mom Aunt Patty didn't neglect us," I say.

"Not if you had fallen off the roof, you wouldn't," he says. And then he wobbles the umbrella he is still holding over our heads. "Then, too, sunstroke is known to hamper the powers of speech something awful."

He holds that umbrella over our heads for the better part of an hour. I guess he would be holding it still but for the fact that the sun went behind some clouds and a little breeze picked up. A little breeze is all Uncle Hob says it is, but it feels pretty gusty up this high. It tried to take the umbrella. "We could go in if that's what you want," he says.

"No, I don't think so," I say. Little Sister shakes her head. She doesn't want to go in either. So Uncle Hob closes the umbrella and gives it to me to hold. Then he scoots back to the window and takes out his guitar to do a little picking.

He picks out a tune I remember hearing before. It's one of those that sound the same over and over, like a nursery rhyme, so I hope he isn't planning to sing it for too long. But Uncle Hob doesn't sing the song, he sings out math problems. Of course Little Sister holds up the right number of fingers. This is more interesting than the song would have been, but after a while, we have all had enough of that. Uncle Hob stops singing and just picks. I don't know what he is playing, but it sounds nice.

21

The Last Straw

I know that sooner or later we will get around to talking about why Little Sister and I are sitting out here on the roof all day. And whether we are ever coming back in. I don't yet know what I will answer to either question. I mean, we have to go in sometime, but it seems more than I can think about just now. I think instead of all that happened before I climbed out here.

After supper last night, Aunt Patty made several phone calls to friends. Or maybe just to people she knew had children at home. "We must be able to find you some suitable little playmates," she said after the third call didn't pan out. She didn't seem to notice that Little Sister and I were not especially eager for her to find us any little playmates.

The next calls she made, she didn't come right out and ask anyone to come over. She asked if their little darlings were home for the summer. Little darlings, no less. Most of them were either away for a while or attending Bible school during the day. Most, because Aunt Patty did come up with one girl about Little Sister's age. They invited us over for the evening.

"This evening?" Uncle Hob could hardly believe it. "On such short notice?"

"It's more or less a get-to-know-you meeting. For the girls, I mean."

"You think they want to see for themselves if the rumors of cannibalism and general terrorism are true?"

This caught me by surprise. Uncle Hob rarely jokes with Aunt Patty. At least I hoped he was joking. As usual, Aunt Patty didn't get it. Or she ignored it. "We didn't have any plans anyway," Aunt Patty said.

"No, and I was looking forward to it," Uncle Hob said. He had a new crossword magazine. He was already deep into the first puzzle.

I tried to side with Uncle Hob. "Liz is coming over later with Robbie and Isaac," I said. "We had those plans."

Aunt Patty acted as if I hadn't spoken. "I think we ought to go on over there for a few minutes, just to say hello and to introduce the girls," Aunt Patty said to Uncle Hob. "We won't stay long."

Uncle Hob gave in. "I warn you, I won't stay longer than an hour and fifteen minutes. That's neither long nor short. It's just right. And it's more than I want to do at all." But he didn't yet put his crossword puzzle down. He printed in another answer.

Little Sister looked at me. I knew that look. I said, "I sure hope she isn't going to be like Cynthia Wainwright."

"Just you worry about being nicer to her than you were to Cynthia Wainwright, Willa Jo," Aunt Patty said. "Then we'll see how things go."

I hated to hear Aunt Patty say that. I thought she knew Cynthia Wainwright wasn't my fault. "I was nicer to Cynthia Wainwright than she deserved," I said.

Aunt Patty didn't even look at me when she said, "Don't be a smart aleck." She was checking her hair in the mirror on the wall near the stairs. There wasn't any bite to it, which in the end was what angered me. She was so sure she could boss us around she didn't look at us when she did it; she didn't raise her voice; she didn't have to pay us any mind at all.

I was suddenly so mad at her I could have spit. I could have kicked holes in walls. I was mad enough to say something mean, but I couldn't think of anything mean enough to say. I turned to Little Sister, who had been listening to everything. I didn't even think about what I did next.

I slipped my fingers into the cuffs of my shorts and snapped them.

"I saw that, Willa Jo," Aunt Patty said in a shocked voice. "Did you see that, Hob?"

Uncle Hob looked up from his crossword puzzle. "What? See what?"

"Willa Jo's making fun of me. She snapped her shorts."

Uncle Hob looked back down at his puzzle.

"Well, thank you very much for your support," Aunt Patty said.

"Now, dumplin'—"

"I don't know what you all want from me," Aunt Patty wailed to the room at large. "My yard is overrun with Fingers. My reputation is in tatters, what with scenes at the

Piggly Wiggly and whatever Lucy Wainwright had to say to her friends. To say nothing of—" She paused, sputtering like she was about to run out of gas. "Why, these children engaged in all-out combat with that Bible school teacher, never mind the ticks."

Uncle Hob said, "Now, Patty, don't get carried away."

Aunt Patty's voice rose to a near shriek. "Carried away? Have you lost your mind, Hob?"

"I might be about to," he said, never looking up from his crossword.

"Nobody, just nobody in this house appreciates me one bit," Aunt Patty said. She paced the living room, waving her arms about to punctuate everything she was saying. "All I'm good for is cooking and cleaning and throwing out those dead june bugs morning after morning—"

Uncle Hob looked up from his crossword.

Aunt Patty stopped and looked at Little Sister, but Little Sister was looking at me. Her eyes were dark with the meaning of Aunt Patty's complaint. "It was only a june bug," I said in a small voice. Not that it would do any good. Little Sister is like Mom; she wouldn't hurt a bug.

Aunt Patty looked just as miserable. "I didn't mean to tell you," she said.

Little Sister turned and ran upstairs. She didn't look back.

"Well, now I've done it," Aunt Patty said. "Why couldn't you just get in the car and go, Willa Jo?"

"Me? You think this is my fault?"

"There is not one cooperative bone in your body—"

"You don't want someone to cooperate, Aunt Patty," I shouted. "You just want everyone to do as they are told."

"Do you see what I mean?" Aunt Patty said. "Willa Jo, I am just fed up with you."

"Then send me home," I said. I went upstairs like Little Sister, but I wouldn't run. I stomped. I was satisfied to know that Aunt Patty watched me all the way up.

I expected to find Little Sister sitting by the window or something. Crying, maybe. But she had gone to bed. She wasn't asleep, but she wasn't crying either. There seemed nothing to do but get ready for bed too. By the time I lay down in the other bed, I realized I was tired enough to sleep.

The only thought I had as I fell asleep, in all her upset and pacing and all, Aunt Patty had never once stepped off those plastic carpet runners.

22

Talking Things Over

When after a while Uncle Hob doesn't get around to asking why we are sitting on the roof, I say, "I guess you're wondering what we're doing out here."

"Oh, well," he says, with a little shrug.

I guess he knows most of it already. About Liz and Isaac, and us wanting to play with them. He knows about Cynthia and Bible school. He knows Aunt Patty is fed up. None of those things take much explanation. The thing is, it doesn't seem right to tell Uncle Hob that Aunt Patty is a problem. So I tell him I don't really care for brown leather sandals. That I like my dirty white tennis shoes fine. That

I'd like to have them back. Plus, Little Sister has a blister on her heel, which she is obliging enough to show him right away. I'm just sorry mine has calloused over.

"Well, getting your old shoes back shouldn't be too hard," he says. "They're up there in the hall closet. Nobody's thrown a thing away."

"I've always worn tennis shoes," I say to explain myself. Also because I don't want him to be mad. Or to hurt his feelings like we've already done to Aunt Patty. He and Aunt Patty have been awful good to us in a lot of ways.

"We'll see to it when we go downstairs," Uncle Hob says. "We'll put a Band-Aid on Little Sister's heel."

I'm feeling some better already, but not better enough that I'm ready to go inside. So I get quiet, hoping there will be no more talk of going downstairs. In fact, there is no talk at all for maybe five minutes. So I am some relieved when he comes up with a subject. Any subject.

"Did I tell you about the summer I was turning thirteen?" he says. "And I was sent off to stay with my grandpa because my gramma had died? My folks had the idea I could be a help to him."

"You were supposed to do the cooking and stuff?" I say.

The thing that crosses my mind right off, how lucky we were to have a garden right outside the kitchen door, and plenty of canned goods on hand. And luckier still, for me, that Mom didn't expect much housekeeping to get done if she wasn't the one doing it.

"Not exactly," Uncle Hob says. "I was there to give him somebody to do for. They figured he would eat breakfast if he had to see to it that I got breakfast. You know what I mean?"

"Like, he would take good care of himself if you were there for him to take care of. I see."

"It didn't work out that way, though. No one had given much thought to how much I missed my gramma. What really happened was we both let things go together."

"What do you mean?"

"We sat around singing funny, sad songs and telling sadder stories," Uncle Hob says. "We didn't wash or cut our hair. Grandpa didn't shave. We ate peanuts and hard-boiled eggs when we got hungry. He let me drink beer. When they came to get me before the start of the school year, our hair had grown to our shoulders."

"It must have been terrible," I say.

Uncle Hob stares off into space, the way he does when he is working on mathematical equations.

"I say, it must have been terrible," I say in a louder voice.

Uncle Hob looks like he is waking up. "No," he says. "I only this minute remembered. It wasn't terrible at all."

23

Aunt Patty Stands Alone

"Hob?"

We hear Aunt Patty calling out the back door. Her voice is sort of distant.

"Hob?" she calls again, sounding even farther away. But she is closer, really, calling from somewhere inside the house.

I look at Uncle Hob. He looks like he has not heard a thing, not one thing, but I know that can't be true. Little Sister is looking at me and her eyebrows are rising like bread.

"Hob?" Aunt Patty calls, and she is coming out through the garage. She looks around, then looks up like she thought of asking us if we have seen Uncle Hob.

"Hob!" Aunt Patty cries, seeing him sitting up here with us.

"Patty," Uncle Hob says in a voice that suggests Aunt Patty is someone he bumped into on a street corner.

"Hob?" Aunt Patty is clearly hoping he will say something to explain why he is sitting on the roof with us.

"Patty," Uncle Hob says as if she has left chocolate fingerprints on the walls.

"Hob," Aunt Patty wails, addressing the world in general. "What am I going to do with this family? Everybody's crazy but me."

"I wouldn't be too sure about that," Uncle Hob says, a smile tugging at one corner of his mouth.

"Hob!" Aunt Patty is suddenly angry. "This is the last straw. The very last straw. What am I to do with all of you?"

"If you can't beat 'em, join 'em," Uncle Hob says. But I can see he doesn't mean it. So can Aunt Patty.

"Are you out of your ever-lovin' mind?" she asks.

"I'm enjoying the breeze," Uncle Hob says. "I'm enjoying the company of two lovely young ladies. I'll be down directly."

Aunt Patty is not going to be jollied out of her mad. She draws in a deep breath, like she might blow us off the rooftop with whatever she is about to say. But then Mrs. Potts calls, "You-oo, Patty." She is coming to visit.

By rights, we all should have noticed Mrs. Potts sooner. We can see anybody coming for miles in most directions. But Aunt Patty held our full attention, right up until Mrs. Potts hollered.

"Oh, no," Aunt Patty moans. "I will never, never live this down."

"Wave," Uncle Hob says, and raises his arm. Little Sister and I do the same, waggling our hands like Mrs. Potts is a personal friend of Santa Claus.

"What is going on up there now?" Mrs. Potts calls out as she approaches the end of the driveway. "I believe the heat must have affected all your minds."

"Our minds are fine," Aunt Patty snaps.

"Hob, tell me something so I know you're feeling like yourself," Mrs. Potts calls.

Uncle Hob sits quiet for a minute. I imagine he's thinking up the right thing to say. Like, "You always sit in the third pew, left side, Sunday mornings in church, Mrs.

Potts." But no. He says in a voice so low even I can barely make it out, "You girls sit still as statues, hear?"

He gets up, steps up higher on the roof, a way behind Little Sister and me, and bows deeply from the waist. His short shirtsleeves flutter gently in the breeze. Down below, Aunt Patty makes a squawky sound. Mrs. Potts gasps. There is even a breathy squeak from Little Sister.

The roof tiles are so hot I cannot set my leg against them for long, turned as I am to watch Uncle Hob. They are only bearable where we have been sitting directly on them. I cannot imagine how Uncle Hob's pale bare feet can stand on them.

Uncle Hob straightens, his arms swing gracefully away from his body, and he starts to dance in this funny, old-fashioned way of bent knees and shuffling feet. His arms are held out to his sides a little. His tie flaps gently in the breeze. He is humming to himself, "Bum . . . bum bum bum, bum," as he bobs and weaves. Little Sister's had a tight grip on my arm since Uncle Hob got to his feet, but now her hand loosens and falls away.

"Bum, bum ba bop bum. Bum de bum bop bum . . ." The tune is not familiar but it occurs to me that there ought to be the sound of foot-tappings or shoe-slidings, at the very least. Maybe an orchestra. He looks so fine in his Sunday best. Uncle Hob is a good dancer.

He shuffles one way, then the other, then turns in a slow circle that draws a kind of sigh from Aunt Patty. Uncle Hob bows once more, differently. Like he is king of the roof. He straightens and says, "I have never felt more like myself, Mrs. Potts."

When I look down to see how Aunt Patty is taking this, she is looking at Uncle Hob in the funniest way. Partly as if she has never seen him before. Partly as if he is the finest of tea sets and he is hers, all hers. Even as I catch sight of it, however, it is a look that is disappearing behind her awareness of Mrs. Potts, who is still beside her.

"Your mother should never have sent you to that college up north, Hobart Hobson," Mrs. Potts says.

"It wouldn't have made a bit of difference," Aunt Patty says. Aunt Patty glances at me and almost smiles. Almost. There is a look in her eyes that I like.

Mrs. Potts puts both fists on her hips like she is prepared to argue the point. But Mrs. Biddle's door opens and she steps out on her porch to call out, "Doris." Mrs. Potts turns to look in that direction.

"Why don't you all come on over for a glass of cool tea?"

Mrs. Potts looks torn.

"We have pound cake," Mrs. Teasley calls from inside the screen door.

"I'm coming," Mrs. Potts calls back.

As the screen door closes, the spring makes a sound like a birdcall. *Brrrrillll.*

Not one word is spoken as Mrs. Potts makes her way down the driveway to get around the fence. We watch her cross Mrs. Biddle's yard where she climbs the steps to the door. There, she knocks politely. The screen door opens and she is sucked in.

"Patty," Uncle Hob says quietly.

"I'm going to sell the house," is Aunt Patty's reply.

"Now, dumplin'."

"Don't you 'now, dumplin' me," Aunt Patty says. "I'm moving to Venezuela."

"Why Venezuela, in particular?" Uncle Hob asks.

"Because nobody there will know me. They will have heard of you and Willa Jo, of course. But they won't guess I'm related. I'll use an assumed name."

Inside the house, the phone rings. We hear it as distant

but urgent. Aunt Patty stamps off to answer it, saying, "Probably want to sell me a newspaper." The screen door slams.

"The front door is seeing plenty of use today," I say, struck with wonder over this entire turn of events. Uncle Hob sighs and seats himself on the other side of Little Sister. He looks a little tired.

"Aunt Patty thought you dance beautifully," I tell him. His face brightens. "Do you really think so?"

24

Aunt Patty Sees
the Light

When we hear Aunt Patty's voice again, none of us are sure where it is coming from.

"Hob?" she calls again.

We all turn to see her peering out the dormer window. Peering, because she must be standing on tiptoe and about the best she can do is see over the edge. She looks like a small animal in its burrow.

"Hob? Are you ever coming back inside here?"

There is something in her voice, something very unlike the Aunt Patty I know. Not sweet, exactly. A little scared, maybe.

"I thought I'd wait till the girls are ready to come in, dumplin'," Uncle Hob says.

"That was their mother," Aunt Patty says, now with a real quaver in her voice. "Noreen called and says she wants to see them."

Uncle Hob doesn't look as if that could be too alarming. "What did you tell her?"

"I can hardly see you," Aunt Patty says, dropping out of sight entirely. "Do you think this rickety old chair will hold me?" she asks. She is already climbing up.

"Don't risk it," Uncle Hob says. He is up in a flash, hotfooting it over the roof tiles. Heat is rising from them in waves that look like ripples on a pond.

Little Sister and I are right behind him. Not that any one of us can do a thing for Aunt Patty. We can only stand there, shifting from one foot to the other, waiting to see what happens. Uncle Hob's eyes are huge behind his glasses as Aunt Patty huffs and puffs her way off that rickety chair to balance on the rafters. Little Sister and I cling to each other like a big wind is blowing.

Aunt Patty never stops once she starts to climb, even though she is not built for climbing through dormer windows. "Now, dumplin', it's not like you're coming out to sit on the porch. You better rethink this," Uncle Hob is saying as Aunt Patty looks for footholds. "I don't think you care for heights. Leastwise, you don't care for them when I get up too high."

"That's because you're accident-prone, Hobart," Aunt Patty says, growing testy as she becomes frustrated with the difficulty of heaving herself up onto the windowsill.

"Me? When have I ever had any accidents?" Uncle Hob wants to know.

"You haven't," Aunt Patty says, "because I watch out for you. I don't know what you would do without me."

"Neither do I, dumplin'," Uncle Hob says, grinning. He reaches for Aunt Patty as she teeters uncertainly on the windowsill, but she slaps his hand away.

"I can do it," she says.

"I wish you'd reconsider," Uncle Hob says.

"I have no choice but to go forward," Aunt Patty says, getting a firmer grip on the edge of the dormer structure. "I can't go backward now."

But when she gets wedged in around the hips and starts to shriek, we all pitch in and do what has to be done. We take hold of her and pull until she pops through, like a cork out of a bottle. There is a little sound of ripping cloth, and

I expect Aunt Patty will get all upset at ruining one of her outfits. But she doesn't mind it. She pats down the tear and says, "No real damage done."

She tries to stand up then. Aunt Patty is too fond of being the boss of things to be comfortable with scooching around. Her foot slides out from under her right away. Uncle Hob grabs for her and pulls so that she sits down hard. "Oh, now, dumplin'," he says, before she has a chance to get mad. "You can't be walking around out here with sandals on."

"Good thing you weren't on both feet, exactly," I say. "You could go right over the edge, looking like one of those skiers up north." I make a little out-and-down motion with my hand.

Little Sister nods.

"This is dangerous," Aunt Patty says. "Haven't I been telling you all this is dangerous?"

"Then why are you out here?" Uncle Hob says with a trace of impatience in his voice. "We aren't going to stay out here forever. We'd be coming back inside directly. Surely you didn't climb out here to tell us that."

"No. No, I didn't," Aunt Patty says. "Don't be mad,

Hob. I couldn't stand being all alone in there. I wanted to be with the three of you, even if we are all crazy as bed-bugs."

"All right, then," Uncle Hob says. He settles us all in a new spot, higher and near the dormer window. Aunt Patty sits and moans, "Be careful now," while we gather up the picnic basket and the empty water jar and the guitar. During all the excitement, the umbrella has rolled into the gutter that runs around the edge of the roof.

"I'll get it," I say.

"No," Aunt Patty shrieks, and I stop.

"Now stop that screaming, dumplin'," Uncle Hob says in a no-nonsense voice. "I'll show you how we can get at that umbrella without even having to take out the ladder."

Uncle Hob shows Little Sister and me this grip he learned in the Navy. You open your hand between the index finger and the middle finger and grip somebody around the wrist while they do the same thing and grip you around your wrist. It looks like shaking hands but what happens is the fingers get a good grip under the wrist bones and it's more like you've tied a knot than like holding hands.

"You can't lose hold of somebody that way," Uncle Hob says. "Even if your hands are sweaty. And if you stay low, gravity works for you too. You're too bottom-heavy to pitch over."

He takes my hand so he and I are gripped together. "We're like a human chain," he says. "Now you're safe as can be, if you want to reach for that umbrella, Willa Jo."

"I'm not quite close enough," I tell him.

But then Little Sister takes my other hand and points at the umbrella. Behind us, Aunt Patty moans.

"All right then," Uncle Hob says. "But you have to stay low, Little Sister. And you and Willa Jo have to hold on to each other like I showed you."

So Little Sister and I twine our fingers around each other's wrist and pull, to show how tightly we've tied the knot. Uncle Hob nods and we stretch down the roof like the human chain Uncle Hob calls us. Aunt Patty's moan becomes a high-pitched keening. Suddenly there is a nervous fluttering in my stomach.

For the first time in most of this whole day, I realize that I have encouraged Little Sister to do a dangerous thing, to sit out here on the roof with me. As careful as I try to be of her most of the time, I have not given that much thought today. It seems like bad judgment on my part. I tighten my fingers around her wrist. It would not do to lose her now.

Little Sister's fingers tremble as she reaches for the umbrella. It is harder for her; she is the one who is close enough to look right over the edge of the roof. In fact, she has been this close more than once today, but I don't think she's been nervous about it till now. It seems likely the sound that Aunt Patty is making has us all keyed up. Then Little Sister has the umbrella and she is scuttling back up to throw herself in Uncle Hob's lap.

Aunt Patty gives in to the urge to cry, and is sobbing loudly.

"Don't tell me you were scared," Uncle Hob says to Little Sister, and follows this with a little laugh. "We were holding on to you."

Little Sister buries her face in his neck. I draw in a deep breath. Everything is fine. Even Aunt Patty's sobs are already drying up.

"You girls have been just fine up here," he reminds us. "You stayed low, you didn't walk around or even move around unnecessarily. You certainly weren't foolish enough to dance. And now you know how to make yourselves into a human chain. Next time I need to fix the roof, I know who I'm going to call for help."

"They're natural billy goats, born and raised in the mountains," Aunt Patty says in a voice that is both tearful and admiring.

Little Sister grins and peers out at me from beneath Uncle Hob's chin. And we all of us agree to move back up by Aunt Patty. "Now tell me," Uncle Hob says to Aunt Patty as he and I settle ourselves with Little Sister between us. Seeing her hanging out over the edge of the roof has had an effect on both of us. Nothing will do now but to see her safely enclosed. "What did Noreen have to say?" Uncle Hob says when we are satisfied that Litttle Sister won't blow away.

"She says she's missing them," Aunt Patty says to Uncle Hob. And then she turns to us. "You girls, she's missing you girls."

My heart lifts at hearing this, and Little Sister's face lights right up.

"And?" Uncle Hob says.

"She said she wants to take them home," Aunt Patty

says. "So I said, 'Well, you can't take them yet.' 'Why not?' Noreen says. 'Because they aren't here now,' I say. 'Where are they,' she says, and I tell her, 'They're out playing.' "

"Somehow I don't think that's going to discourage her," Uncle Hob says.

"I said they were playing at a neighbor's. I said they might stay overnight."

"Oh-h," I groan and let my head drop onto my knees, and Little Sister pats me on the back of my head.

"You can't expect to put her off that way forever," Uncle Hob says. When I look up again, he is looking at Aunt Patty like her mind has flown the coop.

"She's never going to let me hear the end of this," Aunt Patty says.

After a long moment during which Uncle Hob says nothing to comfort Aunt Patty, I say, "We could go downstairs and she'll never know. We won't any of us say a word about this."

Little Sister shakes her head. *No, not a word.*

"Now that wouldn't do," Uncle Hob says. "You can't be keeping secrets from your mother."

Little Sister shakes her head. *No, no secrets.*

"She's coming to get them," Aunt Patty says nervously,

and Little Sister's hand creeps into mine. It is a hopeful hand, I think. "She's driving over."

"Well, good," Uncle Hob says and settles back. "It's like a family reunion."

"She started out much earlier today. She called to say she's coming near," Aunt Patty adds.

"It's time," Uncle Hob says.

"Time for what?" Aunt Patty says. She is sounding more cranky than nervous now.

"Time for her to concentrate on the living," Uncle Hob answers. "She has two beautiful daughters who are still with her. Or who could be."

"It's going to be a disaster," Aunt Patty says, her stubbornness rearing its ugly head.

"It was never a disaster," Uncle Hob says firmly.

"They were living like, well, like every day was their last. Like they wouldn't ever need another dish, so why wash one. Like—"

"Like my grandpa and I lived the summer after Gramma died. You remember me telling you about that, dumplin'?"

"I remember. It was like you were abandoned, like they abandoned you to that old man," Aunt Patty says.

"No," Uncle Hob says. "We only had each other, it's true. But there were things he had to teach me. Things I needed to learn. Things no one else could teach me, maybe, because they weren't able to share their pain with each other."

"What do you mean?" Aunt Patty says.

"I learned that year—just in time, really," Uncle Hob says, almost as if he is talking to himself, "before I started to believe all that baloney about what it is that makes a man—I learned to cry unashamedly. It was the saving of me, really."

"I don't know what you mean by that," I say. But I'm holding on to Little Sister's hand awful hard; I'm that unsure of whether I even want to know what Uncle Hob means. She wiggles her fingers to make me loosen up.

"I might never have learned to cry if it weren't for that time with my grandfather," Uncle Hob says. "I might never have learned to cry. Which means I might never have known really what it is to pray or to laugh right down deep into my belly or to tell your aunt Patty how much I love her."

"Crying is important, then?" I'm suddenly afraid I'm about to cry and I don't even know why.

"Knowing that time is short is important. Knowing to make the best use of it you can, that's important. Letting those around you know you love them. Because you never know when you'll have to say good-bye."

Now Little Sister's fingers tighten around mine.

"All those things are important," Uncle Hob says. "They are the most important things."

Little Sister nods, patting Uncle Hobart on the knee as if to comfort him because she is sitting next to him. Little Sister is the sweetest thing sometimes. Only Baby could ever be sweeter.

The air has gone all quiet. It's as sticky as it has been throughout the day, but it is soothing now in some way that it couldn't be while the sun was right overhead. We all sit together and watch the clouds gather. A trickle of something bright and silvery-white, like melted platinum, wanders across the sky.

"Looks like we're going to get some weather," Uncle Hob says after a while.

"Not till after dark," I say. I don't even know how I know that.

"The crops like a night rain," Uncle Hob says. Aunt Patty sighs. She sounds like she feels the want of that rain herself. There is something I need to tell Aunt Patty, but I'm not at all sure how it will be received.

Instead of speaking directly to her, I say what I must to the air around her. "I'm sorry you aren't going to get into the Ladies' Social League."

"It doesn't matter," Aunt Patty says. "I can get together with Tressa, now that she's moved back to town. And that Fingers woman sounds awfully nice."

"She is. She isn't really having twins."

Aunt Patty straightens her back a little, the sure sign of a new idea. "It might be fun to have her meet Tressa, both of them having all those boys. Maybe we'll just form our own Ladies' Social League. A friendlier one."

"Now there's an idea," Uncle Hob says. Aunt Patty just beams.

"Mrs. Fingers will like you too," I say. "You and Liz are a lot alike."

Aunt Patty actually looks pleased to hear this. "We are?"

I shrug as I say, "You both just say what is on your mind."

"I've been thinking I ought to get to know that girl better," Aunt Patty says. "She's not at all what I expected."

A little silence falls as we all take things in.

"You all think I was wrong," Aunt Patty says to no one in particular. "About a lot of things. I know it. But it's done now, right or wrong. Sometimes these things happen and there isn't one single thing a person can do about it except look back on it."

"That's true," Uncle Hob says.

"Hob," Aunt Patty whines.

"Not a thing, I mean," he says. "That a person can do." Then he grins. "But it's also true, you were wrong."

Aunt Patty gets a sour look on her face that I can almost feel, like it is on mine. In fact, I think that look is on my face sometimes. My voice is quavery as I sing, "I'm a little rain cloud, dark and wet." I suck in a deep breath to sound stronger. "Squeeze me tight and wring me out."

Uncle Hob looks at me like I've gone right around the bend.

But Aunt Patty remembers the words. "Your momma still sings that?"

I nod.

"She made that up when we were girls. Little girls."

"Noreen made that up?" Uncle Hob strums a few notes, then sings it. We all sing it together. All except Lit-

tle Sister, who nods her head from side to side in time to
the melody.

"Oh, Hob, what am I going to do?" Aunt Patty wails.
"She will never forgive me."

"She will," I say.

Aunt Patty and Uncle Hob look at me.

I'm kind of surprised that Aunt Patty doesn't know this
about Mom. "She will. She isn't even mad at Daddy."

"Well, she should be," Aunt Patty says.

"Patty." This is Uncle Hob.

"I know, I know." Aunt Patty settles back. She is trying
to live with being in the wrong, I think. It is not an easy
feeling to live with.

"The house sure did need a good cleaning," I say. But
that doesn't seem like near enough, so I add, "I bet that
firewood is near about dry by now."

Aunt Patty reaches around Uncle Hob and squeezes my
shoulder. But after another moment, she hides her face in
her hands and says, "I just can't stand that all this would
happen to Noreen. She was always the sweetest thing."

I know just how she feels. And Uncle Hob rests his
hand on the back of her neck, like he knows too. But it is
none of it Aunt Patty's fault and I am about to overflow

with feeling for her. I scooch over to sit on Aunt Patty's other side.

"It was awful nice of you to replace those june bugs," I whisper to her. Little Sister might hear me, but this needs to be said. It seems like it ought to be said now.

"That's all right. I only had to do the first one by myself," Aunt Patty says. "Hob helped me with the rest." She leans toward me and whispers, "He caught the fresh ones and tied on their little strings."

I prop my chin on my knees, content that I have cleaned my plate, as Mom likes to say. She isn't talking about food, but about having cleared up misunderstandings and made apologies where they are needed. It seems to me Aunt Patty and I have had our share of the first and neglected the latter. But now I am content to watch the clouds turn and tumble slowly toward us through the heavens.

The sun is behind us now, ready to drop out of sight behind the peak of the roof, but it can still put on a show. Brilliantly colored ribbons stretch across the sky to meet the oncoming gray clouds, making them soft in shades of coral and blue.

Then, like she couldn't stand the quiet another instant, Aunt Patty says, "I'm sorry about all those things I said. I

didn't mean it but for that moment. I love you girls to dis-
traction. It is just an enormous responsibility to . . . well,
you know what I mean. I was overwhelmed. I am just filled
with admiration for your momma. I don't know how she
manages."

I'm not sure this is an apology. "We're good girls."

"Yes, you are," Aunt Patty agrees. "I didn't mean you
weren't. I just meant I should never have been so critical."

I'm satisfied with that. So far as I am concerned, everybody's plate is clean.

"One thing is driving me crazy, and I have to ask," Aunt
Patty says after a few moments, and she is looking at me.
"Whatever made you climb onto the roof?"

It's kind of a shock to be reminded that this is still in
question. It doesn't feel strange anymore that we are all sitting out on the roof. Somehow, the whole dilemma has
slipped my mind completely. "I . . . I wanted to see the sun
rise," I say in a near whisper, because it does not seem to be
an adequate answer. "I wanted to see the sun rise, and I just
stayed."

"You just stayed," Aunt Patty says. She slaps her hands
down on her knees. "You sat up on this roof and baked like
turkeys and now the whole neighborhood thinks we are a

family of lunatics and the only reason you can give me is that you wanted to see the sun rise?"

"We were getting near to Baby," Little Sister says shyly.

There is a moment of shocked silence. Even Little Sister appears to wonder where these words have come from.

Then Aunt Patty says, "Why, did you hear that? Little Sister's done got her voice back."

Little Sister hangs back from this announcement herself. Or maybe she is not as excited about it as the rest of us are. So when Aunt Patty reaches over and envelops her in a hug that includes me and Uncle Hob, Little Sister is looking bewildered by it all.

"Why wouldn't you talk to us, Little Sister?" Aunt Patty says.

Little Sister shrugs, looking like she thinks she is about to be in trouble.

"Don't get me wrong," Aunt Patty says. "I'm real glad you're talking. I'm not mad or anything."

"You sound a little mad," I say.

"Well, I'm not," she says. And now she only sounds tired. "But I'd like to know why. I really would."

She turns her head as if she is staring off into the distance. In a small voice, she asks again. "Why wouldn't you talk to us, Little Sister?"

"I tried," Little Sister says. "I did. But my voice was lost in sadness."

Aunt Patty looks around and there are tears shining in her eyes. Her face is turning pink with the effort to keep them from running down her cheeks. She sort of smiles and says, "We've all been lost in sadness, Little Sister."

It comes just naturally to lean on Aunt Patty the way I would lean on Mom if she were here. The little sound Aunt Patty makes in her throat is welcoming and it seems like we might comfortably sit this way forever. I have a sudden thought. "I don't know how we're going to get you down from here," I say.

"We'll probably have to call the fire department," Aunt Patty says. And laughs. But the tears escape and race each other to her chin.

25

The End of
a Long Wait

The sun is sitting much lower in the sky when Mom pulls into the driveway in the secondhand car Aunt Patty bought. Milly is in the passenger seat. But when Aunt Patty grabs me around the knee with fingers that are bony with tension, I know it is only Mom that she is thinking about.

Milly and Mom get out of the car and Mom walks straight up to the front door without ever looking up. I'm tempted to call out to her, to tell her she isn't supposed to go to the front door. But I can't. And although Little Sister has chattered like a magpie for the last fifteen minutes, she has fallen silent again.

We hear the doorbell. Aunt Patty makes a squeaky sound in her throat.

Then we hear Mom knock. Aunt Patty makes a motion to get up, but Uncle Hob puts his hand on her shoulder and she sits quiet. The movement draws Milly's eye, and she looks up and sees the four of us and puts a hand up to her mouth. But she is quiet.

Then we hear Mom say, "They must've gone to get the girls. Nobody's home."

Milly doesn't say a word. Her eyes are big as saucers.

"Milly," Mom says. "Do you want to go get an iced tea and we'll come back in about a half hour? Milly? What's the matter?"

Mom is walking toward the car as she is talking. When she gets there, Milly says, "Now don't get excited." Then she turns Mom around and points.

Mom puts one hand to her chest and says, "Good heavens."

"It's okay, Mom, we're coming down," I say.

"Right after the sun sets," Aunt Patty says.

"The sun sets?" Mom says.

"You wouldn't believe the view from here, Noreen," Aunt Patty says.

ABOUT THE AUTHOR

Audrey Couloumbis was born in Illinois. The southern voices in *Getting Near to Baby* are voices she's heard all her life. One of her grandmothers came from Virginia and had plenty of relatives there, and the other had relatives that came up from Louisiana. She was a bit younger than Willa Jo when one of her aunts lost a child, and she remembers how the shock of it rocked the family. Although her aunt's baby died of cystic fibrosis, at about the same time, a small child in a neighboring family died of bacterial illness derived from drinking tainted water. It was these memories that sparked the incident around which *Getting Near to Baby* revolves. But also influencing her writing was the memory of the nature of the relationships she had with adults at that time in her life. Like Willa Jo, she had the kind of family whose benign neglect fostered her independence and left her plenty of free time to find her own way in the world.

Currently, Ms. Couloumbis lives in New York City and upstate with her husband. She loves gardening, building stone walls, moving furniture, and driving down roads she's never been down before.